Children of Winter

Illustrated by Ian Newsham

D0335683

BERLIE·DOHERTY

Children of Winter

Mammoth

Also by Berlie Doherty

Tilly Mint Tales
Tilly Mint and the Dodo

for older readers

Granny was a Buffer Girl
How Green You Are!
The Making of Fingers Finnegan
Running on Ice
White Peak Farm

*With thanks to Sue Horner and the young
writers of High Green School in Sheffield,
who showed me the old cruck barn.*

First published in Great Britain 1985
by Methuen Children's Books Ltd
Published 1995 by Mammoth
an imprint of Egmont Children's Books Limited
Michelin House, 81 Fulham Road, London SW3 6RB
Reprinted 1995 (four times), 1996 (twice), 1997 (twice), 1998 (three times)
Text copyright © 1985 Berlie Doherty
Illustrations copyright © 1985 Ian Newsham
ISBN 0 7497 1845 5
A CIP catalogue record for this title is available from the British Library
Printed and bound in Great Britain by Cox & Wyman Ltd, Reading, Berkshire
This paperback is sold subject to the condition
that it shall not, by way of trade or otherwise,
be lent, resold, hired out, or otherwise circulated
without the publisher's prior consent in any form
of binding or cover other than that in which
it is published and without a similar condition
including this condition being imposed
on the subsequent purchaser.

Contents

		page
1.	The Old Cruck Barn	9
2.	The First Day	23
3.	Alone	30
4.	Making a Home	37
5.	Ghost	50
6.	A Gift from Home	57
7.	Theft at Dawn	72
8.	A Meeting in the Woods	76
9.	The End of the Dancing	88
10.	Another Mouth to Feed	101
11.	Candle-light Vigil	113
12.	Coming Back	125

MOORS

Path

Red Berry Bush

RABBIT TRAPS

WOODS

Track

Track

Stepping Stones

RIVER

Hoggs Field

HOGGS FARM

LOWER VILLAGE

TEBBUTT H

MOORS

Blackberry Patches

Boulders

Trickle stream

Track

Catherine Field

BARN

TEBBUTT HILL

Track

Moors and BOULDERS

PATH

Clearing

ROUGH MOORS

RIVER

UPPER VILLAGE

CLEM'S SISTERS HOUSE

USE

For Denis and family

1. The Old Cruck Barn

It seemed to Catherine that from the moment they set out on their journey she knew that it was going to be a very special one. The bus climbed slowly away from Sheffield and up into the hills of Derbyshire, stopping here and there to let on hikers and villagers and people from the remote farms, and every time it lurched forward again on its familiar journey she felt a strange thrill of excitement and dread. She pressed her face against the cold glass and stared out at the green valley now lying far below, at the little clusters of grey buildings that showed only by their smoking chimneys that people lived in them. What was it like, she thought, before they had buses out here? Before the roads were built? People must have spent weeks and weeks in their own homes and fields, never seeing another soul....

'Catherine, we're getting off soon.'

Patsy and Andrew were in the seat behind her, and behind them, Mum and Dad, struggling to fold up the ordnance survey map. Catherine loved that map.

She loved to read the names of the villages and rivers and the hills. Even the fields had names sometimes, like people. Lawrence Field. That sounded rolling and tummocky, with high grasses like fringes round the edges. Howard's Field. That would have huge boulders in it, and the wind would sigh like a long whisper round them. And Catherine Field. That was where they were making for today. Her field.

Andrew forgot his little blue rucksack, and Dad had to run after the bus and thump on the side of it to get it back for him. There was hardly anything in it, anyway, only a small torch and his cagoule, but it had always been a family rule that everyone carried their own belongings, in case they got separated on the walk. Except for the map, of course. Dad always carried the map. It wasn't fair.

He pushed it into his own rucksack now, and zipped up his cagoule. 'It shouldn't take us more than an hour to get down to Gran's house,' he said. 'I don't think we want to dawdle today, kids. It's a bit fresh up here.'

'What about my field, Dad? Aren't we going there?'

'We'll pass it on the way. It's only a field, love. I'll tell you something else your mum and I noticed on the map, Cath, and we never knew it before. See this hill that we have to go down? It's called Tebbutt Hill.'

'Does it belong to Grannie Tebutt? Does it belong to us?' It made up to Andrew for the fact that they hadn't found a field with his name on it.

'No. There's lots of Tebbutts round here. It's a

local name. But it could have belonged to an ancestor of ours, I suppose. Way back in the past.'

He swung his rucksack on to his back and took Andrew's hand. 'Over the stile!' he pointed. 'And follow the path. We can't get lost today.'

Patsy ran on after them. Catherine stood with her mother at the wall, watching the way the path twisted before it plunged out of sight into a dense copse, down and down towards the river in the valley bottom, and Grannie Tebbutt's house.

'Mum, do you think the Catherine of Catherine field was a Catherine Tebbutt?'

'She might have been,' Mum said. 'It would be nice to think that she was, and that you're named after her. What do you think?'

'I think she was Catherine Tebbutt,' said Catherine, but more to herself now, because her mother was over the stile already and picking her way down the path on the windy hill. 'But what was she like?' And even as she thought that she felt again the strange surge of excitement and dread.

'Come on,' Mum called. 'Over the stile and down the path.'

'I'm coming.'

Over the stile, she thought. And into the past.

By the time she caught up with the others they had all put their cagoules on. The sun when it came out was low and brilliant on the September leaves, but clouds that looked heavy with rain soon covered it and brought a bitter chill to the wind.

'We're going to get soaked,' Dad warned. 'We'd better go straight down.'

'I want to do up Andrew's shoe-laces,' Mum said. 'I'll catch you up.'

Dad strode on into the thickness of the woods. Patsy dawdled to pick blackberries, though they were hardly sweet enough yet for eating.

Catherine had found a bush with berries on it as bright as blood. She tried to break off a branch, but the wood was too young and refused to snap.

'What is it?' asked Patsy.

'Don't know,' Catherine said. 'But it's poisonous, I think.'

'What d'you want it for, then?'

'People put it outside their houses to keep away the evil spirits.'

'Do they heck!' scorned Patsy. 'I've never seen them.'

Mum and Andrew had caught them up by now and they hurried on along the twists of the narrow path. Rain spattered down on them through the thinning trees. When they came to the edge of the copse they met with a wind that seemed to come from nowhere and to bring the rain stinging like the lashes of a whip across their faces. They huddled together in the poor shelter that the bare trees gave. Dad was nowhere to be seen.

'Let's go back,' moaned Andrew.

'Don't be daft,' said Patsy. 'I think we should make

a dash for it.'

'Down the hill! But it's miles!' said Mum.

'Well, we can't stay here,' said Patsy. 'We'll drown.'

'We can break away from the path and go over to the left, and down that slope,' said Catherine slowly. 'There's an old barn. We could shelter in that.'

Mum pressed a dripping branch aside to peer down that way. 'Are you sure, Cath? I can't see one.'

'I know you can't. But it's there, I'm sure.' The strange thing was that Catherine had never been so sure of anything in her life, and the thought of it was terrifying. With a sudden increased intensity the rain plunged down between the branches, making their minds up for them, and they all pushed out together, slithering and gasping and half laughing, till Catherine veered away from the path and took them scrambling down a slope of moorland, through dense wet patches of fern and gorse, and, at last, up a steep bank to a low stone wall. Beyond it the grass was short and cropped, and the wall enclosed its small space.

'Catherine field,' she thought.

And they could all see it now, snug in the hollow of the little field. An old stone and timber barn, and the wooden door was swinging open.

Catherine was first in. Triumphant, she held back the door for Patsy and Andrew and their mother. They gasped for breath as they ran in, and tried with clumsy fingers to peel off their wet clothing.

'Well done, Catherine!' her mother said. 'I don't

know how you found this place but it's saved us from drowning, all right.'

'What about Dad?' asked Andrew.

'Serves him right for running on in front,' Mum said; then, seeing his anxious face, 'Don't worry about Dad. He can look after himself.'

She helped Andrew off with his cagoule, shook it, and hung it over a low beam. 'Get your little torch out, Andrew. Let's see what we're doing.'

Catherine had pushed the door of the barn to, so that the only light that came to them trickled through tiny chinks and holes in the roof. Andrew found his torch and flashed it at Mum, who took it from him and played its soft light slowly up and round the roof

and the walls, like an exploring finger. She showed the huge oak beams that were sandwiched together with layers of small stones.

'It's an old cruck barn, this,' she said. 'Very, very old. Look at those cobwebs! They look as if they've been here a few centuries!'

Outside the wind lunged at the barn so that its beams seemed to creak like old bones. Straw and dry leaves lifted and scuttled across the floor.

'I wish Dad was here,' said Andrew. 'Or that we were down at Gran's house.'

Catherine looked across at him quickly, as if he shouldn't have said that. She couldn't explain the odd feelings that were rushing through her now that they were all standing in the barn that only she had known about. Why did the old place give her such a strange feeling of security, and such a terrible feeling of loss? Why did none of the others seem to feel this too? She took the torch from her mother and began to wander round the barn, picking out here and there things that she felt she could name even before the light came to them.

At the far end of the barn was a mound of straw, left there to dry over the winter. 'Straw, for sleeping on,' she said. 'Bins for the food.' Her torch found four old tubs leaning, empty, against a wall, and then moved over to a large, flat-topped boulder. 'The table,' she said.

Andrew stared at her. He had caught her odd mood before the others, but had no idea what to make of it. 'Mum, what's the matter with Catherine?' he asked.

'She's play-acting,' said Patsy. 'Just ignore her.'

Catherine didn't seem to have heard her. She moved over to the other wall and felt along it till she came to a window.

'That's it,' she said. 'The window. But these shutters should open. I know they should.'

She dropped the torch as she struggled to push open the shutters, and the light dimmed quickly. Mum picked up the torch and shook it.

'For goodness sake, Catherine, you've nearly broken this thing. What *is* up with you?'

'Let's go, Mum,' said Andrew. 'Let's find Dad. He'll think we're lost.'

'If he's got any sense he'll have gone straight on down to Gran's,' Mum told him. 'He'll be tucking into her ham sandwiches any minute....'

'He mustn't go to Gran's!'

'Catherine ...!' Her mother's voice was warning. 'You've gone far enough,' it said. 'I've had enough of this.'

Catherine swung away from her. How could she expect her mother to understand, when she herself didn't? 'He shouldn't go there, Mum,' she muttered.

'He wouldn't leave us all behind,' Andrew reminded her. 'He might be looking for us ... and he'll be all wet.'

Their mum knew when she was beaten. She picked up her wet cagoule and slid it back on. 'I don't know,' she said. 'Kids!' She handed the torch back to Catherine. 'Careful with this,' she said. 'It's nearly broken as it is with your messing about. If I don't see him up in the woods, I'm coming straight back. And don't let any strangers in....'

The wind rushed in to meet her as she opened the door, and, as if she was taking the sound and the chill of it with her, softened again.

Catherine wanted to run after her mother. She struggled to pull herself out of the strange feeling of sadness that those last words had brought to her.

'I wish she hadn't gone, Patsy,' she said.

Patsy, although she was younger than Catherine, was far more practical. She was like her mum.

Catherine's dreaminess was beginning to annoy her. Dopiness, she would have called it. She could see, however, that it was beginning to alarm Andrew. She led him to the mound of straw that was heaped up, higher than their heads, across the back of the barn, knowing that he would obligingly tumble about in it, like a young dog.

'It's lovely and warm in here,' she said. 'Like a house.'

'You ought to try spending a winter here,' said Catherine.

'I don't like it much,' said Andrew.

'It makes a good shelter, anyway,' said Patsy.

And the word 'shelter' clutched at Catherine again. It was almost as if she was remembering.... 'People did shelter here. About three hundred years ago ... people ... children ... lived here.'

'It's got ghosts,' whispered Andrew doubtfully.

'Yes,' agreed Catherine. 'It has got ghosts.'

'Don't, Cathy,' sighed Patsy. 'You'll frighten him.'

'It's only pretend,' Andrew said, to comfort her.

Suddenly Catherine knew how she could bring out these strange thoughts that were lurking half in her mind, half, it seemed, in her memory, and that were struggling like trapped fishes to be allowed to float free.

'Pretend!' she said. 'Let's pretend!'

'Hooray!' shouted Andrew.

Patsy scowled. Pretend! 'Pretend what?' she asked in spite of herself.

'Pretend it's three hundred years ago. Sixteen – sixteen hundred and something. And we're three children who've come up here to spend the winter.'

The wind came with a slam against the side of the barn, and then hushed into silence.

'All on their own?' said Patsy, scornfully.

'They wouldn't,' said Andrew. 'Not without their mum and dad.'

'But they had to,' Catherine insisted. 'Or they would die.'

Again, the wind shrieked round.

'I know!' Patsy entered at last into the game as she remembered a recent history lesson at school. It had been about a tiny village in Derbyshire that had cut itself off from the rest of England in 1666. 'It was because of the plague.'

'Oh Patsy,' whispered Catherine, suddenly more frightened than she had ever been before. 'It was. It was because of the plague.'

She moved away from them, and as she did so the light of the torch faltered and dimmed. Andrew felt for the comfort of Patsy's hand.

'A long time ago,' began Catherine, just as if she was telling them a story, as indeed she was, at first. 'On a day just like this, in autumn, three children came up from the village to spend the winter in this barn.'

'But they wouldn't...' began Andrew.

'They had to,' Patsy reminded him.

Catherine stopped. Was it a story she was telling?

She seemed to know, and yet not to know. She seemed to picture that walk as if in her memory, struggling against the wind with bundles of clothing and sacks of food. Over three hundred years ago.

'Let's pretend...' Patsy prompted her. A game of any sort would be better than seeing Catherine in this odd mood.

'Right. We're three children who've just come up from the village. I've put all our food and clothing over in this corner for the time being. Our mother and father will be coming soon.'

'But you said we'd be on our own,' Andrew reminded her.

Catherine frowned. She didn't understand that part herself yet. Surely the children's mother and father would come? She decided to leave that bit for the moment.

'Andrew, you're very excited about coming here.'

'Am I?'

'Pretend you are, anyway. You've been here lots of times before, on your own, because you know the shepherd who sometimes stays over here when the ewes are lambing. You come to see him.'

'What can he be called?'

'He can be called ...' Catherine frowned. 'I know what he's called! It's Clem.'

'Clem!' shouted Andrew, delighted. He could imagine Clem now. He could imagine running in to the barn to find Clem crouched over a ewe in the straw pile, in the low light of a lantern swinging from one of

20

the beams. Clem would have looked up, pleased to see him. 'Tha's come in good time, boy,' he would have said. 'See the lamb, in the hay there?' Andrew would have picked up the little thing and cuddled it in his arms. 'T''is for thee to nurse,' Clem would have said to him. 'Give it milk from the bowl on the tip of thy finger. And gentle, mind!'

'And you're not called Andrew,' said Catherine, breaking into his daydream. 'You're Dan. You're Dan, now.'

'Dan. Am I six?'

'Yes. And your leg is hurt because you fell over on the way up the hill.'

'Pretend I stopped to look after him,' broke in Patsy, because that's exactly what she would have done.

'But she's not called Patsy, is she? Give her a name,' insisted Andrew.

'She's Tessa.'

'Tessa!' Patsy tried the name, and liked it. 'All right. I'm Tessa. And what will you be called?'

'I think ... I think I'm still called Catherine.'

It was then that Catherine knew for sure that she wasn't making up stories, or pretending. She was remembering. She was remembering the day when another Catherine Tebbutt of her own family had stood in this very barn with the wind howling round and the rain hammering down in just the same way as it did today. 'Catherine Tebbutt.' Her brother and sister were again awed by the strange tone in her voice.

They could see her face lit up oddly in the last light of the dying torch, and they saw how tense she was, and how far away was the look in her eyes, as though she was already moving in a different time. But they were drawn in now, trapped. They wanted to be there, too.

And then the torch-light died.

'Catherine, the light's gone out!' said Patsy, alarmed, but this time it was Andrew who reassured her.

'It doesn't matter,' he said. 'It's time for the game to start. We'll go outside, shall we?'

He dragged Patsy towards the door and ran out, too excited to worry about wrapping himself up against the weather.

Catherine stared at the door that slammed shut behind her brother and sister.

'Aye,' she said. ''Tis time.'

2. The First Day

The boy and girl struggled up the last slope of the hill. He was limping a little, and every so often bent down to touch his knee. His sister held his other hand and half-pulled him with her. They were anxious to get to the barn away from the sharp bursts of wind and rain that bullied them from all sides, it seemed; yet they were apprehensive, too, at the thought of having to face what had to be faced. Yesterday their mother and father had brought sacks of food and all manner of bits and pieces from their cottage up to their barn, and had returned to them weary and worried. They had been warned to go to no one's house, to speak to no one, to keep to their own yard, and that was all. And now, today. Mother had sent them on with their older sister, and had told them that she and their father would come up to the barn to join them when they had finished sorting through their belongings.

But how sadly she had pushed them away from her, and how desolate their home had seemed, with all their possessions gone.

As they came up the last slope towards the little

field they knew as the top field the boy started to run, remembering his earlier journeys to this very barn to see his shepherd friend Clem, and to help him with the new-born lambs. Those had been better days than this. For a moment he forgot his knee and brought his sister running with him.

'Clem may be here. He's my friend,' he said, and shouted 'Clem! Clem!' as he always did. He pushed open the barn door eagerly and in came his sister after him, laughing and panting for breath, and she swung the door to, behind her.

It was dark in the barn, except for a light in one corner, and that made the darkness seem even deeper. The light moved towards them, and they saw that it was the light of a candle, and that their sister Catherine was carrying it. For a second the other two stared at her, surprised to see her like this, looking as if she had made the barn her home. The hem of her long skirt was damp with mud from when she had crossed the lower stream in the bottom field near their farm. She clutched her shawl round her against the cold that they had brought with them.

' 'Tis time an' all. Clem be'ent here, Dan. But what a pair of tortoises th'art! Leaving me to do all the work – 'tis right good, that.'

'I fell, Catherine!' Dan explained. 'See where I cut myself!' He rolled back the hem of his trouser carefully to show his knee glistening with the ooze of blood and smeared with dirt. Catherine bent down to touch it, and he winced away from her.

'Tessa stopped to help me,' he added through his tears.

Catherine smiled up at him. 'Did she now? Well then, Tessa can bathe it for thee, an' all – there's a trickle-stream round back. But get dry clothes on first – there, on the straw. I've laid them out for thee.'

Dan glanced at Tessa, then struggled out of his shirt and trousers and put on the rough woollen and sacking clothes that had been brought up for him. Catherine put his wet things on a low beam at the back of the barn while Tessa changed into the long black skirt and warm shawl that were ready. As she put her apron on she found a clean square of white linen in one of the pockets, and she knelt down to have another look at Dan's sore knee.

''Tis nothing,' she pronounced. 'Muck. That'll soon be gone.' She spat on the cloth and rubbed on his knee, ignoring his squeaks. 'Don't fuss, donkey.' She laid the piece of cloth on the wound and bound it tightly round, too intent on making sure that it didn't slip down again to show much sympathy.

Catherine was deep in her own thoughts. It was as if she had a worry inside her that was too dreadful to be told. She lodged her candle in a crack in a large flat-topped boulder. The crack was made up with wax, as though it had been used many times before for the same thing. Dan tried to remember whether he had ever seen the old shepherd Clem do this. He wondered if it was Clem's candle that Catherine was using.

'This can be our table,' said Catherine. ''Tis just the right shape, and smooth as wood.'

Outside the wind was moaning, but it was dry and sheltered in the barn. Now that they were used to the light Dan and Tessa could see that the barn was really quite big, and that the strong beams that bound it from end to end made it look as solid as their church. About a third of it was taken up with a huge mound of dry straw. Blankets from their beds at home were laid on them. So they were to stay the night, then. They hadn't even known that. Lined up against one wall were some wooden bins, and these were crammed full and overflowing with apples and vegetables, cheeses wrapped in cloths, salted meats, and cakes, oats and barley. Dan ran to rummage through them, excited again.

'See these,' said Dan. 'There's food for a feast here, Catherine.'

His sister slapped his hand as he reached into one bin for an apple. 'Nay, not for a feast, and not for thee, mouth, so leave it!'

'Then who is it for, Catherine?' asked Tessa. 'Isn't it from our house?'

'Aye, it is. Father brought it all last night before he went to see Gran Tebbutt.'

'But why so much, Cath?'

'Because ...' the older girl sighed. How could she tell them what she didn't know herself for sure? Why couldn't they guess as much as she had done? 'Because, I think, 'tis to last for a long time. Weeks.

And weeks.'

'Everything's going funny,' said Tessa. 'Everyone in the village seems sad and frightened. All since the Baker children died. People stay in their houses, and no one comes to talk. Mother and Father keep secrets from us. Mother cries, I know she does, and Father does nothing to comfort her. And now we come up here – are we to live here now? And why?'

Dan stared from one to the other of his sisters, not daring to interrupt their big talk. This was the mood he had seen in his parents, when his mother kept still and quiet by the fireside, and his father stopped his singing.

'Don't ask me,' said Catherine. 'I don't know.' She sank down on to one of the blankets, overcome now with the day's tiredness. It would be a relief at least to share her worries and her guesses.

'I think something terrible is happening in the village, but I don't know what it is. There is sickness, and there are more deaths than in the Baker's house, that I do know. I think Mother and Father want us all to get away from it, if we can. Hide from it, if such a thing is possible. . . .' Catherine faltered. 'Whatever it is.'

'But they are coming, aren't they?' whispered Dan, at last. 'We won't be here on our own?'

'Of course they're coming, little man.' Catherine drew Dan down on to the straw next to her. It was coarse and sharp through the fabric of his clothes, but after the long haul up from the village in the rain it was comforting enough.

'That's all right then,' he said. He stuck his thumb in his mouth and wriggled down inside the blanket. ''Twill be all right, when Mother and Father come.'

How easy it was for Dan to fall asleep.

After a while Catherine went outside to look for her mother. The wind came in so fiercely when she tugged open the door that it would have blown out the candle if Tessa hadn't jumped up to shield the flame with her hands. Catherine closed the door as gently as she could, and climbed up the little slope of the field. She crossed over the stretch of moor to the edge of the woods, and to the path that plunged down and round rocks and ferns into the depths of the woodlands. Far below that, and out of sight behind the trees, lay the village that they had left hours before. Already daylight was dimming.

Catherine cupped her hands round her mouth. 'Mother!!' she called. 'Mother!' But the wind tossed her voice away from her so that even she couldn't hear it, and below her the great trees crashed their branches together in the storm's fury. The colours of autumn showed up in all their intensity in that strange wet light. A few yards below her Catherine could see a bush with berries as bright as blood. She clambered down to it and snapped off one of the branches, then made her way slowly back to the barn. By the door there was a large boulder. She climbed up on to it and pushed the end of the branch as far as it would go into a crack between two of the small stones that made up part of the wall of the barn.

'There!' she said. 'Tha can keep away now, evil spirits! We want none of thee here.'

The wind mocked her with its great roar, so that even as she jumped down from the boulder the berries were torn from the branch, to drop one by one to the ground. Maybe some berries still clung to the small twigs that were cupped in the little hollow that she'd found for them. Catherine didn't have the heart to look. Rain spat from the dark sky.

Catherine was thankful for the lull that came as she opened the barn door, and for the dry warmth of the place, and the kind light of the fluttering candle. She tiptoed past the straw pile where Dan and Tessa were lying quietly, and hung her wet shawl on the low beam to dry.

Tessa murmured, half-asleep: 'Has she come, Cathy?'

'Not yet.'

'Are tha afraid?'

Catherine knelt down by her sister. 'Nay,' she said softly. 'And nor must Tessa be. Mother will come. She said she would.'

She sat by Tessa a little while, then crept over to her own blanket in the straw. She lay listening to the light breathing of her brother and sister, and the sound was so comforting against the cruel moan of the wind that very soon she gave in to it, and, like them, fell fast asleep.

3. Alone

It was the sound of fierce banging on the door that woke Catherine. She stirred slowly in her unfamiliar bed and gazed up at the sunlight pushing its thin fingers of light through the holes in the roof. She closed her eyes against the brightness and listened again to the banging, trying to remember where she was and why she was lying in a blanket wrapped round with straw. On one side of her was Tessa, coughing slightly as she too began to waken, and on the other side was her brother, fast asleep still, and by the sound of it still with his thumb in his mouth and sucking back the dribble as he always did.

The knocking persisted.

'Catherine!' a voice called. 'Catherine! Open the door, child!'

As soon as she recognised her mother's voice Catherine threw back the blanket and ran to open the door. They were to be all together again; that was the only thing that mattered.

Her mother was sitting on the boulder that would

come to be known as the sitting stone. She had a large bundle at her side, wrapped round with rope, and by the look of it it had been dragged, not carried, over the stepping-stones where the river was at its broadest, and up along the muddy path, and through all the dying leaves. Tied to a tree at the side of the barn was one of their farm cows, Cloudy – Tessa's cow, and their favourite. It made everything all right again to see Cloudy away from home as well.

'Mother! What kept thee so long?' Catherine ran to hug her but her mother jumped up to stand away from her, with the boulder between them.

'Don't touch me, Cathy!'

The girl half-laughed in her nervousness, and stared at the change in her mother. She picked anxiously at her skirt. Her mother's face was pale and streaked with tears. She wore her shawl wrapped tightly round her, as older women did, so that it covered her head. It made her look old and ill. For some reason a picture came to her of her mother scooping grain from a bin to throw to the hens, and laughing because the day was bright, just like today. That had not been long ago, when sunshine made people happy.

' 'Tis something bad, then. Tell me.' And now all the dread of yesterday was rushing back to Catherine; leaving the farm with their mother bravely smiling at them down in the bottom field and their father on his way to Granma Tebbutt's house.

'I will tell thee, and 'tis just as terrible as tha says.

But I'll not come inside. Be brave now, and I'll tell thee.'

Catherine couldn't look at her mother any more. She looked across at Cloudy, moving her head and tugging at the eating-grass in that familiar way of hers, and that was some sort of comfort.

'So...' she prompted.

'I went to Granma Tebbutt's at first light this morning,' her mother said. 'I wanted to leave some things for her, and to bring your father here with me. She is very ill. She has a fever.'

Again Catherine said nothing, and neither did she turn her head to look at her mother.

'Tha father has been nursing her all night. How could he have left her, his own mother? When I saw him he was half dead with tiredness and worry. He had to rest, and I could not leave her or him wi'out seeing to them. And that's it, Cathy. Tha should know now what it is that makes Granma so sick. 'Tis the plague.'

The plague. So that was it. And hadn't she known this all along, too, in her heart of hearts? That was the word that no one spoke in their village, though there wasn't a soul who hadn't heard of it, and who hadn't prayed in dread for the people of other villages who had lost so many men, women and children, and whole families at that. No wonder people had kept their mouths shut, and kept only their fear in their eyes, when the Baker children died and cottage doors stayed closed. How many more had there been? And was Granma Tebbutt to be the next?

'Tha father and I hoped to get away in time,' her mother went on. 'That was why we planned to move up here to the barn, just our family. We thought we would be safe enough here till the plague had done its worst and burned itself out. 'Twas little enough to ask for, to save a family. We could have managed here.'

Tessa had joined Catherine in the doorway now, rubbing the sleep and the sunlight from her eyes and wondering what it was that her mother could have told her sister that could have subdued her into such a cold silence. 'Are we to come back home, then?' she asked, just catching her mother's last words. 'Have I to waken Dan?'

'No!' her mother said sharply. 'I know him. He'll come running to me wanting to touch me. Let him sleep there till I've gone.' It was not easy for her to keep her voice steady. They could both tell that.

'I'll go back down now, girls. On my own, see? Tha father must stay with Gran, to do what he can for her. It's too late for him to leave her now. And I ... must run the farm till he can come back home to it. And Tessa and Cathy ... th'art to stay here.'

'But not on our own!' gasped Tessa. Catherine put her arm round her.

'I'm asking thee to be brave, child. There's food and shelter and clothing here.'

'But how long...?'

'When 'tis safe, I'll come and fetch thee home. And if anything has happened to me, that I may not come for thee, then a messenger from the village will come. But let no one else in till that messenger comes. Promise me.'

And the girls promised, knowing that only one thing would prevent their mother from coming for them herself. 'See here,' she said brightly, 'I've brought up things from home that tha father and I intended to bring up anyway today. 'Twas already wrapped, so tha can be sure I've not touched it since I went to Granma Tebbutt's house.'

Catherine shuddered to think that already her mother might be carrying on her garments and on her skin the traces of that terrible disease that cost so many people their lives.

'I've dragged it up the hill on this rope. Tha should have seen me, Tess. 'Twould have made thee laugh to see me carting this thing along, and bringing all the stones of the path along with it. Now Cathy, you're to leave this out here, and open it with care, using sticks, and when th'ast the little things from the bundle, then burn the blanket it came in. Understand?'

Catherine nodded.

'And there's Cloudy, look, Tessa, for the daily milk.'

Tessa had always milked Cloudy. She ran to her now and nuzzled her head against the cow's warm, creamy-white side. Cloudy swung her head round and lowed softly.

'I'll not come up here again, girls. I dare not, till I know that all is safe with Father and me. Be busy,

34

then tha'lt not be sad. God help thee. I want thee to be safe.'

Again the three were silent.

'Don't let anyone in. Promise me that,' their mother insisted.

The girls nodded, knowing that they were so far from anywhere here that if anyone came to that barn it would be from their own village. And if they were not bringing them news of the end of the plague, then they would be bringing them the plague itself.

'Then I'll go,' said their mother. 'If there is anything to be left for thee 'twill be on thy side of the river. But never, never be tempted to cross that river. Promise me.'

Again they promised, never imagining how hard it was going to be for them to go to the bank of the river and to look across from there to the smoking chimneys of their own home, and yet to stay away.

'And if any of thee start with a fever, come home. Goodbye, girls. Be strong.'

Yet still their mother did not want to go.

'Mother, wait, th'can see him!' Catherine suddenly guessed her mother's thoughts. She ran inside the barn and pulled back the stubborn shutters that covered the window at the far end so that sunlight fell on to the pile of straw that had been their bed and where Dan still lay sleeping. Their mother looked in for one brief second at her youngest child, and then walked rapidly away. Catherine closed the shutters again, knowing that she would never want the of her mother's stricken face as she had peered in then.

When she went outside again their mother had gone. Tessa and Catherine climbed up the banking at the edge of the field to look down towards the wooded slope. They could hear the sound of her running feet for a long time, and occasionally they saw a branch bend as she pushed it aside, but they didn't glimpse her again. They still couldn't believe what was happening to them, nor could they imagine how they were going to survive alone in that rough shelter.

'We'll be all right, though, Catherine, won't we?' Tessa asked her sister doubtfully.

'Of course we will,' said Catherine, not looking at her but at the path that their mother had taken. 'We'll manage, Tessa. We'll have to.'

4. Making a Home

There was plenty for them to do that day to take their minds off the things that their mother had told them. They let Dan wake up in his own time, and told him nothing till he asked them why their mother wasn't there. Tessa told him as much as he could understand. He cried when he heard how ill Granma Tebbutt was, and that his mother and father weren't going to join them in the barn but were having to stay down in the village instead.

'And now I've a surprise for thee,' said Tessa. 'Come outside, and tha'lt see it.'

She led him out to where Cloudy was tethered and he ran to the cow and rubbed her neck as he did every morning of his life.

'There now, 'tis not so bad with Cloudy here.'

He believed Catherine when she told him that everything would be all right, and from then on he didn't seem to worry about the possible dangers of their new life, or to pine for home. If he did, he learned to keep it to himself, just as his sisters did.

Behind the little field that enclosed their barn the moorland rose up steeply to a high Edge, with huge boulders and sprawling bushes of gorse and bramble, and, here and there, tall trees where crows gathered. It was just where the boulders became the far wall of their field that the children found the tiny crack of a stream that Catherine had already christened the 'trickle-stream'. Here it splintered from rock to rock, and for a time it ran underground. Eventually it would reappear and thicken to join the broader stream that ran down to the river in the valley: their river.

Tessa cupped some of the water into her hands and rubbed it into Dan's face.

'Hold still, muck-tub,' she said as he squirmed away from her. 'Tha's still got all the grime of yesterday on thee. Let's see that knee of thine, now.'

She wiped away the last of the caked blood and dirt from the sore, then washed the piece of cloth that she had used for a bandage under the trickle-stream. 'I'll put it to dry, just in case,' she said. 'But there'll be no need of it because no one is to have any more sores or hurts again. Promise!'

'Right, Tessa,' promised Dan, who had realised already that he wouldn't get the sort of sympathy from his sisters that he was used to getting from his mother, so would prefer to keep in one piece anyway. He scampered away from them, thrilled with the novelty of playing again after so many weeks of being cooped up in their yard at home. He scrambled over the boulders behind the barn to trace the course of the trickle-stream back uphill. Minutes later he came running down to them again, arms striped with scratches, lips purple, cheeks swollen.

Tessa ran to him in alarm. 'Now what?' she scolded.

He held his hands out to show her his find: fat, sweet blackberries all squashed together in his hot palms.

'Where did tha get these?' marvelled Catherine. The three of them were stuffing the blackberries into their mouths so they burst, and the sharp juices trickled down their chins.

'Behind this field. 'Tis full of them!' said Dan.

'Good,' said Catherine. 'We'll eat blackberries while they last, then, because the apples will keep a long time yet.'

She had planned that they would eat bread and fruit while the bread lasted, and then start on the cheeses and the meats. Most of the vegetables would keep for weeks and could be eaten at any time. Dan found a mug which must have belonged to Clem and raced off to fill it up with blackberries for their next meal, and to fill his stomach with twice as many as this, even. When he came back to the barn his hands and lips were stained purple and his stomach hurt, but the girls had no sympathy for him.

'Tha'll be full of grubs and maggots, too,' Catherine warned. 'And if tha eats many more tha'lt waken tomorrow with a purple face, and tha nose as fat and squashy as a berry.'

Dan didn't care. He tipped his mug of blackberries

on to the table-stone and ran off to collect more.

'Tessa, let's sort the apples out, shall we?' said Catherine. They lined one of the empty bins with dry straw so that the apples could lie in it between layers and not touch each other. They would keep better that way. Tessa put all the good apples into one pile and Catherine put the bruised ones into another.

'What do they remind thee of, Tessa?' she asked. Tessa shrugged.

'These bruised apples remind me of people diseased with the plague. Having to keep away from healthy people in case they spread it.'

'Don't, Catherine.'

'I would like to tip the whole lot over the mound so they all go rolling down the hill and into the river.'

'Well, do it,' said Tessa. 'But think, Cathy. If those bad apples are like people with the plague then these sound ones are like us. When we wrap them in straw to keep them fresh and good we're doing what Mother did when she sent us up to the clean air away from the village.'

Catherine knew that her sister was right, and that they couldn't afford to lose all these apples anyway, so she dealt with them lovingly and wrapped the bruised apples separately to be used first, and when it was done she pushed the bins over to the cool end of the barn. She loved the smell of apples, and for many years to come she would remember it, sweet and sharp as it rose to greet them every time they came into the barn.

*   *   *

Later Catherine busied herself outside. She hung all their damp clothes on the low branches of a tree, because with the passing of last night's storm the day was bright and warm, with a good breeze blowing. She thought with a pang of her mother's line of laundry outside the farmhouse at home – sheets and linen cloths flapping like huge light-winged birds, and the smell of them as they were lifted down again at the end of the day. She went back slowly into the barn and looked at the bins that were yet to be sorted: grains into one, meats and cheeses into another; and vegetables to be separated, too. There seemed so much – yet how long would it all last? Long enough?

'Catherine. Can tha come?'

She could hear Tessa and Dan laughing breathlessly outside, and when she joined them it was to find them struggling to bring a huge log over the slope of the field.

'Look what last night's wind has brought down!' Tessa shouted.

'We've dragged it for miles!' panted Dan. 'Come and help us, Catherine.'

'What's tha want that thing for?' asked Catherine. She felt angry with them because they seemed to be enjoying themselves and she felt they had no right to be happy. All the work she'd done that morning, and all they could do was play!

'We're taking it into the barn!' said Tessa. 'Help us, Catherine.'

She beat them to the door and stood with her arm

across it as though she were defending her barn with her life.

'We want no trees in there!'

'Yes, we do. We want to sit on it, don't we, Dan?'

'But we have straw for sitting on, and plenty of it!' Catherine was laughing in spite of herself at Dan's attempts to ram her with his end of the log.

'Then we must have a log for sitting and thinking on. Oh, say yes, Catherine, 'tis such a nice log!'

Catherine had to agree that it was a nice log.

'See, it even has a bulge at one end that looks like a cat! 'Tis a right good log for any house.'

So Catherine gave in, and even helped them, still protesting, to push the log up against the wall of the barn, close to the table-stone. Tessa and Dan both sat on it and tried to look comfortable. 'Ah, 'tis good,' sighed Dan, stretching out his legs as he had seen his

father do after a long day in the fields. He drew back his sore knee and began to pick bits off the scab, as though this was exactly what the log had been brought in for. ' 'Tis right good, this!'

'We can sit and think on here when we've spent the day busy working,' Tessa said. 'Come, Catherine – try it.'

Catherine perched herself between the two of them. ' 'Tis a good thinking-log,' she agreed. 'But it must not be used for thinking sad thoughts. When that happens we must do as Mother said, and be busy. Be busy. And thee, scabby little boy,' she added suddenly, jerking out her elbow so that she knocked Dan off his end of the thinking-log, 'can fetch us some of those berries tha picked, and some bread, and water from trickle-stream, and we'll feast.'

*   *   *

The feast was little enough, though Mother's bread was still good to eat, and sweet with malt. But it put off for a little longer the task that was still to be done and which lay like a weight of sadness just outside the door where it had been left that morning. It was a job that had to be seen to however much they dreaded it. They must unpack the bundle that Mother had dragged up the hill for them. It would contain things from home. It would contain memories.

'Come on,' said Catherine at last. ' 'Tis best we do it now.'

They were careful not to touch any part of the bundle with their hands. They managed to loosen the knot of the rope with twigs that they broke from their thinking-log, and then to draw back the folds of the blanket and lay them flat. Now they could handle the contents. There were some smaller rugs, and Cloudy's milking-pail. Inside the pail was a jug and some bowls, a lantern, many candles, and a slate. Wrapped in its own cloth was the family Bible. Many evenings would be spent at the table-stone with Tessa and Catherine carefully reading from the Bible, and teaching Dan his letters from it to copy down on the slate. And that was all. There was precious little after all to remind them of home, though in time to come they would notice where the edge of one of the rugs had been carefully patched and mended by their mother, and when they came across certain stories in the Bible they would hear again the sound of their father's voice, and see his rough hands nursing the book as he bent towards the firelight at home to read from it.

They carried the bits and pieces into the barn. Catherine put the lantern and the stock of candles on to the table-stone.

'These candles are precious,' she told Dan. 'Think. If the flame goes out, how could we light it again? We would sit in darkness, and this barn would never be a home to us then. We must never, never let the candle blow out, or burn right down.'

Dan, round-eyed and solemn, promised never to let the precious flame go out. Even he understood that the light and warmth from the candle had turned the dark, damp barn into something like home.

Very carefully, Catherine put the lit candle inside the lantern. 'Now we must have the burning,' she said. ''Twill be like an offering.'

She thought then of the red berries she had pushed into the crack over the door, and of the evil spirits that must lurk in the woods below the field and in the stony cliffs behind it. And she knew that she must keep the thought of these to herself.

She made a taper by twisting a long piece of straw, and lit it at their candle. The other two followed her out and they stood in silence as she lit each end of the rope. It smouldered slowly, unwilling to burn as it was so thick. It stung their eyes with acrid smoke but they were reluctant to move away from it. It seemed that they were destroying their last link with home. At last a spurt of flame licked round the rope and Catherine dropped it on to the blanket, as her mother had told her to, and kicked the twigs that they had used on to the pile. Choking smoke curdled round them. Maybe that was why Catherine's tears flowed so freely.

'What a sin, to burn a good blanket like that!' moaned Tessa in Granma Tebbutt's voice, trying to make her sister smile. 'It makes my old heart grieve!'

It was Dan who broke her out of her sad mood, though. The feast seemed long ago, and he suddenly realised how hungry he was.

'We can make a cooking-fire here!' he said. 'Let's cook some potatoes on it!'

He found some small stones to wall in the coil of rope and the burning blanket, and the girls, pleased to have something to do again at last, found dry twigs and sticks piled in the sheep-pen at the back of the barn. Dan carried three potatoes from the bin and washed them at the trickle-stream, and then he put them inside the fire with stones holding them in like a little oven. He had seen Clem do this, and had shared such a meal with him, breaking through the blackened skin and scooping out the sweet mush inside. They piled sticks round it, and soon the bonfire blazed. It was wonderful to feel the heat of it on their faces and arms, and to hear the rush and crack of the flames on the dry wood. And Tessa still had her favourite job to do.

'Come, Cloudy,' she said. ''Tis our time.'

She found a small boulder to squat on, and fetched the milking-pail, and then brought the cow over to the spot. She pulled at the udders till the spurt of creamy milk started and became a steady jet. 'Twist and pull, twist and pull, till our good pail be brimming full.' She leant her head on Cloudy's side and gently sang the song she always sang to her, and it seemed to her that everything was all right, after all. When the pail was full she led Cloudy back to crop the sweet grass by her tree, and brought the jug and bowls out of the barn, along with the linen straining-cloth that her mother had sent up. Carefully she poured the milk through the cloth into the jug. The milk frothed as it sloshed from the pail, and was as warm as her skin where it splashed her. She filled three bowls and carried them over to where the others were sitting by the fire.

While he had been waiting Dan had been running backwards and forwards across to the far woods to collect more fallen twigs and branches to store away and dry in the pen. He had never worked so hard before, but every time he came back to the field he rewarded himself with a few blackberries, even though by now his stomach was groaning.

And at last the potatoes were cooked.

They were better than Dan had hoped they would be, even. The girls had never tasted potatoes cooked in this way before, and watched as Dan split the baked and cracking skin. Hot steam rushed out. Inside the skin the potato was soft and sweet, and as creamy as Cloudy's milk. Dan looked at his sisters expectantly as they sucked out their first mouthful.

'Ah, hot!' gasped Tessa.

'But good?'

'Aye, right good. We must tell ... we *will* tell Mother to cook them this way!'

It was the first year that they had grown potatoes, as they were new to this part of England. They seemed a strange vegetable, and Catherine's heart had sunk when she saw so many of them in with all the turnips and the other roots.

'Aye,' she echoed, when her mouth was cool enough. 'We will tell Mother.'

The fire was settling down, logs crumbling into ashes, small flames purring. They could hear Cloudy chomping contentedly by her tree. Already the light was dimmer, the sun growing pale and watery.

' 'Tis hard for me to think that we've been here a whole day,' said Tessa. 'This morning all I wanted to do was to lie in the straw and cry. But I've been too busy to find time to do it.'

'Good,' said Catherine. 'It must always be like that. If any one of us looks sad, they must be given work to do.'

Dan groaned. 'But not tomorrow, Cathy. Tomorrow I want to play. I think I've had enough of being busy.'

'Tha can look for more blackberries. Tha likes doing that.'

'I don't think I like blackberries as much as I used to.'

'Then we must all go into the wods to collect more

logs and branches for the fire. Yes, Dan, we must. If it rains soon we won't have wood that's dry enough for burning.'

'Good,' said Tessa. 'That must be our job for tomorrow, then. Wood-collecting.'

Their fire was almost out now, just flakes of white ash with a red glow in the centre. They went back into the barn, which felt warm and welcoming after the chill that had crept up outside. Yet with the light from the one candle it had a sort of bed-time gloom that encouraged first Dan and then Tessa to snuggle their blankets round them in the straw.

Catherine sat on the thinking-log for a long time, watching the flame dance on the candle and the long shadows leap across the walls and the raftered ceiling of the barn. She was thinking of Tessa's words out there in the firelight. Yes, they had got through today all right, and they would get through tomorrow, and the next day, and even the next. But what then? Could they ever think of the barn as their home? 'Soon all we'll want to do will be to go back home again, no matter what happens to us,' she thought. ' 'Tis all I want to do.'

She thought of her mother, sorrowing and poised for leaving them so many hours ago in the field outside the barn, and she thought of the promise she had made to her to keep them all there till word came for them that it was safe to go back home.

'Please God, help me to do that. Help me to keep my promise.'

5. Ghost

Dan woke up suddenly in the night and knew that he could hear a ghost. Someone was walking in the straw, making it crackle. He lay for a long time looking at the candle-flame shadows on the ceiling. When his eyes had grown used to the gloom he struggled up so that he was leaning on one elbow. The ghost of course was invisible. He had expected that. But the ghost had made a sound, and that sound was near to him in the straw, and it made his flesh grow cold.

Now that he was awake he was aware of the pains in his stomach again, brought on as he well knew by blackberry greed, and he knew that he must go outside to the place in the trees that Catherine had told him he must always use. The thought of going out of the barn into the cold, dark night was bad enough, but knowing that he must first move across the path of a ghost was much worse. He lay propped on his elbow for as long as he could, with his eyes straining into the darkness and his ears straining into the quiet until he couldn't bear it any longer.

'Ghost!' he shouted. 'Ghost, go away! We have no fear of thee!'

Immediately the ghost ran across the floor. He could hear its light footsteps. His sisters woke up.

'Dan! What's happened? Did tha dream badly?' asked Tessa.

Dan had pulled his blanket round him so that only his nose showed.

'I frightened the ghost away,' he whispered. 'Has it come back yet?'

'There's no ghost, shiver-shoes,' Tessa told him. ''Tis in thy dreams.'

'No, I was awake when I heard it,' he insisted. 'I woke up because I wanted to go to the place in the trees, and then I heard it walking about in the straw. And when I shouted it ran away. I *heard* it, Tessa.'

The three sat up in their beds in the straw and listened, but there was no sound.

'Get thee off to thy place in the trees,' said Catherine, 'and then perhaps we shall all sleep.'

She lit another candle for Dan to take outside with him and when he came back she blew it out so as not to waste it. Who knew how long their candle-store would last? She cut three pieces of bread and ladled milk from the pail for them all. Dan hurried back to his bed and lay like a fish between the two girls, trying to get himself warm again, and they ate their late feast.

'How much bread do we have left?' asked Tessa.

'Plenty. Enough for two weeks or so yet.'

'And then what?'

'Two cakes with fruit in, that will last. Meat and cheese. Potatoes. Plenty.'

'And what happens when 'tis too wet for us to light a fire to cook the potatoes in?'

'We eat them without cooking them.'

'Oh Catherine!'

'Don't ask me, then. No more questions about tomorrow and after that and that. It doesn't help us, does it? We must always think just about today; what we do today.'

'I quite liked today,' said Dan, snuggling down again with the bread and milk comfortable inside him. 'Today was better than I thought it would be.'

'We made a fine fire, didn't we?' Tessa laughed.

'We cooked fine potatoes, and that was even better,' said Dan. His thumb was in his mouth again; they could tell by the way he said it. The two girls lay down again and slowly drifted back to sleep.

Dan opened his eyes first, then Catherine, then Tessa. They could all hear it now. Behind them the straw rustled. Someone was moving with quiet care across it.

' 'Tis here again,' whispered Dan.

'I know,' whispered Tessa. 'I can hear it.'

'I don't believe in ghosts,' whispered Catherine.

'Nobody can hear ghosts,' said Tessa.

'I can,' whispered Dan.

The crackling started up again. The three lay with their eyes wide open in the dark, not daring to speak, hardly daring to breathe.

Tessa touched Dan's arm and breathed somewhere near his ear, 'Tell it to go!'

Together they sat up and shouted, 'Go away, ghost! We have no fear of thee!' and they heard the ghost's light feet scamper across the floor.

Catherine leapt from her blanket like a hare from its hole. She ran to the lantern and held it high, swinging its light across the floor and walls. Then she grabbed her boot, and flung it at a corner of the barn.

''Tis not a ghost!' she sobbed. ''Tis rats!'

'Rats!' Tessa screamed. She jumped off the straw and hugged her blanket round her. 'Rats! Rats!'

'Rats!' Dan curled himself down into his blanket. 'That's good. I thought it was ghosts.'

And after all it was neither rats nor ghosts, but a field mouse that had sneaked in through a crack and had come into the straw for warmth. Tessa and Catherine calmed down again when they saw how tiny it was. They were well used to mice, but rats, they knew, brought disease. It had even been said that rats brought the plague.

By this time they were wide awake. There was no point even in trying to get back to sleep. It was no longer dark anyway; already daylight was thrusting its way through the chinks, and outside they could hear the birds carrying their morning song from tree to tree to tree.

'We must sit on the thinking-log,' Catherine said to Tessa. 'And talk about the ghost.'

'But it wasn't a ghost, Catherine. It wasn't even a rat, though tha terrified me when tha said that it was.'

'I terrified myself. But I think the little mouse was more frightened than any of us.'

'Then what is there to talk about?'

54

Catherine sat with her head in her hands, trying to think what it was that their mother would say to them now.

'Mother would say . . .'

'That we were foolish as hens to be frightened of a mouse,' suggested Tessa.

'She would tell us that we will be frightened of many more things while we are here, and mostly it will be because she and Father aren't here to comfort us. But she would say that there can only be the wind and storms and animals coming to frighten us. We must be brave about things like this.'

'Catherine. What if it had been a rat?'

'Then perhaps it would only be coming in to shelter from the cold.' But Catherine shuddered. She knew that wasn't it. She knew the rat could bring death. But there was something else as well. What would Mother have said if she thought it had been a rat?

'The food! We must cover up the food!' she gasped. 'That's what Mother would do, Tessa. Then the rats won't smell it or come to steal it from us.'

'Perhaps we should keep it off the floor. Could we use those low beams as shelving to put the bins on?'

'And we must block up the cracks with pieces of twigs and little stones. That will stop them from coming in at all.'

And it would stop that new fear, perhaps. Facing the fear. That was something new to think about, too.

'Poor little mouse, I like him,' said Tessa. 'We could keep him.'

'We could not,' said Catherine firmly. 'If we find him again he goes outside where he belongs.'

'He's in the straw with me,' came Dan's voice from inside his blanket. 'He's all right, now. He's my friend. I think I'll call him Ghost.'

6. A Gift from Home

There was plenty for them to do over the next few days. They lost count of the time, and soon of the day itself. They ate when they were hungry, and once a day they lit a straw taper at their precious candle and used it to make a fire of twigs on the hearth they had fashioned. They cooked fat potatoes on it, which they ate sometimes with slices of salt beef, and sometimes with cheese. There was always milk for them, and water from the trickle-stream where they washed their bodies and, sometimes, their clothes. But once the weather became too damp to dry things they stopped washing their clothes, and grew used to the smell. They stopped washing themselves too, except for their faces in the morning, and their hands when they were too mucky to eat with.

Every day Dan collected blackberries, though he soon learnt not to eat more than his share. He had to wander further and further afield to gather them as the month wore on, and they began to lose their sweetness and plumpness. He found mushrooms sometimes, which Tessa would cook on the little slab which they wedged into the side of the fire, and which came to be known as the cooking-stone. They had to take it in turns to cook the food on the stone, because the bitter smoke hurt their eyes when the wind blew it towards them, and their arms became mottled red when they held them too close to the heat; but Tessa had a knack of being able to turn the food so that it didn't scorch, and so that none of it was lost in the flames. She could draw the mushrooms back just before their moisture was lost, so that the juice from them oozed when they bit into them.

'Like slugs,' said Dan, looking at them swelling on the slab.

'Aye, but good ones at that,' laughed Tessa.

One morning Dan came to them with his pockets stuffed with chestnuts, still in their spikes. With great triumph he piled them on to the table-stone in front of Catherine.

'What are these things for?' She was annoyed at being interrupted from her task of counting out the candles they had left. Stumps of burnt-down candles lay in a heap at her feet waiting to be scraped and melted down one day.

'Why, they're for eating, Cath,' he said, surprised. 'The trees are dropping them now. Soon the woods will be heaped with them.'

'Well, I'll not eat them. My mouth would bleed.'

'Why, thou *ninny*!' How could his sister know so little? 'Split the case. Look!'

He drove the point of a knife down into the green shell and exposed the chestnut inside. He cracked the brown skin with his teeth and peeled it away to show the nut, white as a bone. 'Bite this!' he said.

'Can we not cook them,' she asked, liking the taste. 'Ask Tessa.'

So that evening a handful of chestnuts shared the cooking-stone with the potatoes, and the pulp of them was every bit as sweet.

Gathering wood for the fire took up most of their day. They soon used up all the dry logs that Clem must have stored away for his own use in the pen. New wood was hard to break into usable lengths, and if it was young it bent rather than snapped, and when it was put on to the fire it smoked rather than burned. The nights were so damp now that every day their hearth was sodden. It was Tessa who had the idea of bringing straw from the barn to light the fire with. The first time they did it the straw that they carried out blazed and burnt away before the flames had even touched the logs. She brought more, and again the straw leapt into flame and died before the logs were caught. She was close to crying with frustration.

'We'll use up all our straw and have to sleep on the ground tonight,' she moaned. 'And still these potatoes won't be cooked.'

'Well then, leave it,' said Catherine, who hated to see her sister in this mood. Tessa's high spirits were important; Catherine needed them more than her sister knew.

So they ate their potatoes raw that night, and didn't think much of them.

Catherine saw to it that all the cracks and holes that she could reach in the barn walls were filled in with pebbles and twigs and even folds of leaves. She pushed the bins against the bigger ones. It was a long, tiring job, and took her days to finish off properly, but it seemed to her that the barn was warmer already.

'That will keep the draughts out, as well as the old rats,' she thought with satisfaction, and knew that she'd done as good a job on this as her father could have done. She couldn't reach the roof of course, and every morning they woke to see the sun pushing its yellow stripes through the cracks in it and they were glad of this. They weren't so happy when it rained, and they could feel as well as hear the dismal plopping.

'At least we can wash us here without going down to the trickle-stream!' Tessa laughed, and would push Dan and hold him under the leak because he was the grimiest of them all, with his forages in the forest.

One afternoon Dan was sitting at his slate, drawing. He was perched on the sitting-stone by the door, in the little bit of watery sunlight that the day had left. Tessa was milking Cloudy, and Catherine was inside the barn cutting meat for the night's meal.

'Tessa,' whispered Dan.

'What is it?' Her voice was dreamy, as it always was when she milked Cloudy. It was something to do with the warmth and softness of her side, that perhaps reminded her of leaning against her mother at bedtime, when their father read to them or recited ballads; and it was something to do with the rhythm of her task: 'Twist and pull, twist and pull ...'

'Tessa!' Dan said again, because his sister was very nearly asleep at her work.

'I hear thee,' she murmured.

'When did tha last go down to the river?'

That brought Tessa out of her day-dream. 'Th'ast not to go down as far as the river – tha knows that right well, Dan.'

'Not as far as the river. Just to see if Mother had left anything for us. Catherine tells me to look when I go to the woods. But there's never anything for us, is there? I couldn't help it, Tess. I only went down as far as I dared, and then I thought something looked strange.'

'What?'

'It was something about the cottages behind Mistress Hoggs' farm.'

'But tha can't see the cottages from there, Dan. All tha can see are the chimneys smoking.' Catherine had joined them outside now.

'Then how many cottages are there, Catherine?'

'Why, tha know'st how many. Fifteen, at that side of the church.'

'So I thought,' said Dan. 'But there were but seven chimneys smoking. That was what looked strange.'

*   *   *

It was too late that day to go along the path, as it would soon be too dark to see anything, but the next morning Tessa and Catherine went down together to the edge of the woods. They looked beyond Hoggs' farm towards the cluster of cottages of their own part of the village. Dan was right. There were only seven chimneys smoking. Yet however hard they tried, they couldn't tell whether theirs was one of them.

But then Catherine spied something that drove the first dread away from her. 'Tessie! There's something for us! There's a bundle.'

She dropped the armful of sticks for the fire that she'd been gathering on the way down, picked up her skirt hem and ran down to the river, with Tessa sliding down the banks of wet leaves behind her.

The bundle had been left right on the edge of the river, close to the stepping-stones, and when they came to it they could see that it was a loosely covered box that had been dragged across the stones on a plank. Tessa ran forward to pull back the cover, and Catherine grabbed her arm to hold her back.

'No, Tessa! Don't touch it!' she warned. 'It may have something of the plague on it.'

She remembered how her mother had shrunk away from her in terror of passing on anything of the disease to her children. 'We'll lift the cloth away with sticks. That will be how Mother put it on, tha can be sure. We must take as much care of it as she did.'

So they lifted back the cloth inch by inch, though Tessa was dancing with impatience and excitement.

62

They laid the cloth to one side, and then carefully lifted up the layer of straw that covered the contents.

'Eggs!' Tessa sat back on her heels, disappointed. Catherine lifted the corner of the wad of straw to reveal more eggs underneath. They could tell that straw and eggs had been lifted up together from the poultry yard. The box smelt of their yard at home, and some of the eggs had brown feathers stuck to them, fluttering bravely like small flags.

'No cakes. No bread!' moaned Tessa. 'How could Mother not have baked for us?'

'How could she bake for us?' snapped Catherine, though her own throat was tight now. 'She would have to touch the flour with her hands to bake, and to breathe over it. How could she bake for us!'

'And no clothes! I wanted more warm things.'

'We have enough,' Catherine answered her. But she knew that Tessa was right. Already they slept with all their clothes on and with all their blankets covering them. She remembered the weaving that she had helped her mother with over the summer, best wool dyed blue. It would be for new cloaks and bonnets for them, she had promised. But it was said that the plague in that other village in Derbyshire had been caused by a basket of fabric sent from London. Their mother would take no chance like that with them.

There was something else that she looked for. She searched in vain through the layers of straw and round the box that contained it.

'What else is there?' asked Tessa.

'Nothing. I thought there would be a message for us, but there is nothing. No tidings. Why?'

Their mother could neither read nor write; she wouldn't have known how to leave a message. But their father could, as could the children. Surely he would have chalked a few words on a slate for them? But there was nothing; and as the tears welled up in Catherine's eyes she knew why there was nothing. There was surely only one thing that could prevent their father from leaving word for them.

'I think perhaps Father is too ill to write to us,' she said at last to Tessa. Both girls fell silent, so that the lonely curlew's cry way up on the moors was the only sound that could be heard.

'Cathy! Tessie!' Far away, and tiny, came Dan's voice. They'd forgotten about him. He had been in a playful mood that morning, more inclined to climb trees and to chuck cones and nuts down at them than to collect wood, so they'd come down without him.

'Shall we eat these eggs, then?' asked Tessa. 'Let's take them up and cook them, unless tha wants them raw.'

Their mother and father always swallowed their eggs raw but both girls hated them that way. It would be like swallowing cold slime.

'This plank is good for burning, and we should destroy this cloth, too,' said Catherine slowly. 'Dost think we could manage it up to the barn?'

'But how, without touching them? We could take the cloth and the sticks, but never the plank.'

'Pity. It would make a lovely fire.' She turned to the box of eggs, then said, 'We could cook them down here!'

'How could we light a fire here?' Tessa shouted, venting all her useless anger on her sister. She would rather have had nothing at all from home than this.

Catherine sat down again. The emotions and the disappointments of the morning were more than she could take now. Why were there so many problems? Nothing was simple any more. If Mother and Father were here they would think up the answers for her. She was tired of having to think of everything for herself. She didn't know if she could go on doing it for much longer.

What she did know was that she didn't want to go back up to the barn just yet. She wanted to stay down here as near as she dared to her own home, and to cook the eggs that her mother had sent for them.

The answer came to her all of a sudden. She let it out slowly so that Tessa would see how good and obvious an answer it was.

'We can bring down the lantern from the barn, with the candle alight in it!' she said. 'Bring it carefully, so we don't lose the flame, as 'tis all we have. We will light a fire here from that.'

'But it will take hours for us to go all the way there, and to come all the way back down again.'

'Tessa! Please!' Catherine wished she was Dan, six instead of thirteen. She wished Tessa was the oldest. 'Please!'

'Very well,' said Tessa at last. 'Am I to fetch some roots, and the bowls and spoons, too?'

Catherine didn't answer her. Just do it, Tessa, she thought. Just do it without asking me.

Tessa knelt down by her. She saw now how tired and unhappy Catherine was, and her sudden flare of anger drained away. 'Why, Catherine, tha looks all in! Tha can sleep, perhaps, while I fetch the things. Dan can help me. And look, I'll get too hot, running up this hill and down again, like a tinker's dog. Shall I leave thee my shawl, look, and tha can sleep on it. No, I know tha'st no mind to sleep – rest, I mean. And see 'tis still warm for me when I come back down again.'

With that she took off her shawl and rolled it up like a cushion to go behind Catherine's head, and without looking to see how wearily her sister sank back on it, ran off up the hill to the barn.

And it was while Catherine was deep in her weary sleep that her mother came creeping across Hoggs' field to stand at the very edge of the water that separated her from the girl. She had heard Tessa's and Catherine's voices and had watched them as they had scampered excitedly down the hill to the box of eggs that she had left for them. Now she wanted to go up as close to them as she dared. She would have loved to cross the stepping-stones and to sit by Catherine till she woke up, and to ask her how they were managing up there on the hill. At the very least she would have liked to call across the water to her. But she knew that the sound of her voice would bring Catherine running across the stones to her, in spite of all the promises they'd both made, and she knew also that if Catherine came to her she'd want to hug her and bring them all back home. So she contented herself with looking as long as she dared, and when she heard the high and happy voices of the other two way up on the hillside she ran back into the shadows of the tall trees at the far side of Maggie Hoggs' field.

Perhaps Catherine dreamt about her mother, because she woke up refreshed and contented when Dan and Tessa came down to her. They soon had the cloth and the plank blazing inside a snug hearth of stones that Dan put together, and they broke their eggs into bowls so that they all sizzled when they stirred them round, and the bright yellow yolks clouded and glazed into the white. Dan had found some chestnuts on the way down and they prised them open and laid them on the stones too, so they would soon scorch and pop. It was a good meal, and it was good to sit so near home to eat it.

Unknown to the children they were being watched by two women. One was their mother, hiding, and the other was Maggie Hoggs, the owner of the farm. She was watching them from the window of her low-roofed cottage at the side of the field, drawn by the sound of children's voices drifting happily in the farm's silence. But the sound brought no happiness to her. She had nursed all six of her children and seen

them die over the last few weeks. The first had been
Tommy, the little one, the same age as Dan; his
friend. The other children had gone before she had
time to mourn, and now she knew that her husband,
lying in his bed of fever, was beyond praying for.
Must she sit in her silent home and wait for her own
time to come? Must she be plagued like this by the
sound of children's voices?

She had listened to them long enough.

They heard her shouting to them before they saw
her, so intent were they on the business of eating.
When Catherine saw the cloaked figure stumbling
towards them she started up, thinking at first that it
must be their own mother.

''Tis well for thee, 'tis well for thee!' the woman

was shouting. 'Tha's come to haunt me, has tha, or to mock me with tha laughing?'

'Why, Mistress Hoggs, 'tis I, Catherine Tebbutt. What tidings has tha of my mother and father?'

'What care I for thy mother and father? What care I for anyone who lives?'

Now the children could see the rage that she was in, and they looked at each other with dread. What could have turned their old friend into a screaming witch like this?

''Tis well for thee, hiding up there in the hills! I know thee. And why should tha be saved, tell me that, when all mine died? Why should the Lord spare thee, and take all mine?'

She flung herself into the river, not waiting till she reached the stepping-stones, and ploughed across it, thigh deep in the murky water and with her long robes flowing like billowing wings around her. She held her arms out to the children as if she would embrace them and drag them all down with her. Dan clung to

Catherine in terror, but Tessa ran forward to help the poor woman to the bank.

And that was when their mother came screaming to them out of the trees.

'Don't touch her! Go away, children. Go!'

And she too ran to the very edge of the river and waded in after Maggie Hoggs, who was stumbling now in the strength of the current.

'Mother!' shouted Tessa, and would have jumped in, too, if her mother hadn't again called to her to go away. She had grabbed hold of Maggie Hoggs by now and was dragging her back to her own side of the river.

'Go, children!' she begged. 'This woman is mad with grief. She doesn't know what she's doing. She's lost all her children in the plague, God help her.'

'Call thysen a Christian, and hide tha children, would tha?' shouted Mistress Hoggs. Her voice and her face seemed years older than the children remembered; she was another woman, and a strong and terrifying one at that as she struggled to free herself from their mother's grip.

'Let me touch them. Let me breathe on them the breath my children breathed on me!' She shook herself free and again plunged down into the water.

'Tessa! Catherine! I beg thee, go. She will harm thee for sure in her madness!'

The girls stood as if frozen with fear. Dan broke away from Catherine and ran screaming to the river's edge, and Maggie Hoggs would have had him in with her if Catherine hadn't darted forward and grabbed him. She started running back up the hill with her face hot with tears that she didn't even know she was shedding.

'Come on, Tessie!' she shouted. 'Bring the lantern. Come!'

And Tessa, torn between her mother's wishes and her own, mesmerised by Mistress Hoggs' madness, stood watching the two women struggling together half-in and half-out of the river, till her sister's voice carried down to her at last, and she snatched up the lantern and followed her up through the woods and out of sight of the farm.

7. Theft at Dawn

The children went straight to their beds that night. They all slept fitfully, remembering from time to time that terrible scene by the river. Dan cried to go back home, and the girls cried in their hearts for their mother. Catherine was wide awake long before daylight. She sat for a time on the thinking-log, listening to the other two in their unhappy sleep. It was bitterly cold that morning, and when she went out to the trickle-stream for drinking water she found that it was frozen. The sky was white by now, and would remain so all day. Rooks and crows bunched themselves together on bare branches. They croaked bleakly to one another. Truly winter was here.

Catherine thought it would be an idea to light their cooking-fire just inside the little low pen that had been built on to the back of the barn, and where they stored their logs. It had no roof, but at least the walls would provide a shelter from the wind. But they should keep Cloudy in the pen perhaps, and bring straw out of the barn for her. How would they feed her when the grass was frozen into the ground? And if they gave her the oats and corn that they themselves ate, would these last her till the thaw? And if they kept her in the pen they would have to fashion some sort of roof for it, perhaps out of logs. That would keep her dry. But how could they light a fire in there if they did that?

There seemed to be no answer to these problems.

Coming back into the barn, and thinking again, as she would do from time to time for weeks to come, of the events of yesterday at the river, she remembered that they had left the box of eggs behind in their haste. She told herself, then, that that was what she was going back down for, but she knew too that if she didn't go back to the river-bank soon she'd never rid herself of the nightmare memories of what had taken place there.

She decided to let Tessa and Dan sleep on, though there was as much daylight now as there would ever be on that gloomy day. She ran lightly down through the woods, and her steps rang on the hard earth, and her breath danced in front of her. Better to set off on a task like this than to sit brooding all day on the thinking-log. That was forbidden, but there was still plenty of it done.

As soon as the path brought her at last out of the woods into the clearing she could see the black gleam of the river and the slow rise of smoke from Mistress Hoggs' chimney. Soon she could see the egg box, and could tell even from there that it was turned at an odd angle, and that straw was lying round it. She ran down the last part of the slope to the river, but she knew now what she would find. The box had been turned over. All its contents were scattered. Every one of the eggs was smashed.

In her frustration Catherine would have liked to kick the box, straw and all, shell fragments and all, into the river, and would have done if she hadn't remembered that the broken eggs would provide food for some hungry animals that would find little else to eat now the ice had come on the earth. She looked across at the closed-up shutters of the farmhouse, and the pigeons perched in their loft. She looked at the yard, empty except for the hens scratching round it. A picture came to her of Maggie Hoggs on market-day, with baskets and baskets of eggs to sell, and her children playing round her. Plenty of eggs to sell then; plenty of people to buy them. But what use had that poor mad woman for hens now?

Almost without realising it Catherine had crossed the stepping-stones on to the other side of the river, and was creeping across Hoggs' field. Her heart leapt like a wild bird in her throat. She sidled across the field like a cat, as slowly as she dared. It seemed to take her hours to cross it. Not a sound came from the house. When she reached the yard the hens ran over to her, standing on her feet and pecking the hem of her dress in search of grain. Catherine shrank away, not daring to move, hardly daring to breathe; too frightened either to go on forward or to run back. From inside the cottage came the sudden shriek of a bench being scraped back, and that brought the life back into her. She bent down, grabbed two hens, tucked one under each arm and ran back over the field like a thieving fox.

8. A Meeting in the Woods

Days passed, maybe weeks. The cold became more intense. The children had to force themselves to leave the shelter of the barn at all. Wordless, they walked with their sleeping-blankets wrapped round them, doing the tasks they'd set themselves, and still they were cold. At night they clung to each other for warmth. Dan cried a lot these days, and even Tessa's spirits were down.

And the ground under Cloudy's tree was as hard as iron. There was no feeding for her there. They brought her into the pen, and pushed the biggest logs against the side of it to lean against the barn wall, making a kind of sloping roof. Dan had the task of bringing straw from the barn out for her. It was Dan, then, who made the find. He came rushing out to the pen with his news.

'Tessa! Cathie! Come quick! The barn is full of sheep!'

'Sheep!' Catherine believed him, because it was at this time of year, surely, that Clem would drive his flocks down from the upper moorland to give them winter shelter. She marvelled that they hadn't seen the shepherd before now.

'Well, quick then, before they eat our beds!' The two girls ran into the barn, laughing, and stopped short at the door.

'Where, then? There's no sheep here!'

'Dan! Not a ewe to be seen!'

'Not live ones,' he explained. 'Dead sheep!'

'Where, in the name of goodness?'

'Why, in the straw, under where we slept.' And, grinning at his trick, he pulled back a layer of straw. 'There.'

He was right. Stretched to dry between layers of straw were some whole sheepskins. 'But I don't know how they got there.'

'Clem will have put them there, ready to sell at market.' Catherine picked one up, shook the straw from it, and draped it round her shoulders. She hugged its warmth to her body.

'Must we wear them?' Tessa asked. 'They smell!'

'Aye, and so dost tha! Of course we must wear them. They're warmer than those blue cloaks mother was making for us. Look, one each, to keep the frost from our bones. And we can cut the other to make leggings.'

'We'll look like sheep ourselves,' said Dan. 'Clem will drive us down the hill when he sees us here.'

And that was a new task for them. They spread the spare skin on the floor and dragged their knife across it, tearing it then into rough shapes to tie round their feet and hands. When Tessa dressed Dan up in his he charged round the barn on all fours like a young lamb, proud of the find he'd made and pleased with himself for making his sisters laugh again; and warm, at last, for the first time for weeks.

'But won't Clem mind?' Tessa worried. 'We shouldn't really cut these up without asking him.'

'If he came here he would give them to us,' Catherine promised her. They took her word for it and revelled in the warmth the skins gave them day and night.

They were ready, then, for the day that the snows came. They woke up to it one morning, and could see in it the tracks of the animals that had prowled round their barn in the night and had kept their distance. It hushed the distant howl of wolves and the dry cackle of the crows; it seemed to cloak the field with quiet and comfort. And after the snowfall came sunshine and blue skies, though the snow stayed firm on the ground and the air was cold enough to freeze their breath as it left their lips, or so it seemed.

Dan was ecstatic about it. He whizzed handfuls of snow up into the branches of the trees, or through the barn door, when it was open, and at the hens.

Tessa marvelled at the new loveliness of their trees. 'Sing hey for the wind! Sing ho for the rain! And sing for the gentle snow again!' She sang in the field at the top of her voice till a well-aimed snowball filled up her mouth.

'Why, Daniel Tebbutt, thou toad-faced goblin, I'll have tha head for a snowball, see if I don't!'

Catherine sat on the thinking-log listening to their

screams of laughter as Dan and Tessa chased each other round the field. She wondered sadly how long it was since they had last played like that. And had she lost her childhood then, in all this, since she couldn't run out and play with them? Yet she felt some kind of comfort in the snow – surely it must curb the plague? Whatever it was that carried it from house to house wouldn't survive this cold. She was much happier, too, about their survival, especially now that they had the warmth of the sheepskins on their backs and round their feet. They had plenty of apples and nuts to feed on, and some salt-beef, though they hated the sight of that now. The stolen hens weren't very good layers, but they did supply them with a few eggs every week, and she loved the familiar sound of them as they fussed round Cloudy in the pen. And if Cloudy's milk was thin these days, she was warm and comfortable to lean against, and she smelt wonderfully of home.

They had found a way of building up their hearth and cooking-stones, so now that the air was dry instead of damp they could make fires again, and cook thick broths of barley and vegetables to warm themselves with before they went out collecting sticks.

' 'Tis not so bad, this,' she thought.

'Here, Cath. Some milk.'

Surprised, she looked up to see Dan's hand pushing a bowl through the door. It was brim-full. As she went over to pick it up she saw that it was full of snow, not milk, and when she ran out to throw it at Dan she was met with a barrage of snowballs from both sides.

'Right!' she shouted, scooping up snow as fast as she could and forming it ready. 'I'll get thee. And when I do, tha'll have snow in tha mouths, and down tha necks, and right inside tha new sheepskin leggings an' all!'

And shrieking with laughter, the three raced round the barn and pelted each other.

'Catch, catch, catch me if tha can.'

Tessa was the one who was being chased. She broke away from the others and raced across the stretch of moor between the field and the woods, and, elated, continued running until she was further into the woods than she had ever been before. She leaned against a tree to get her breath back and saw a brown unfamiliar shape lying on the patchy snow. It was a rabbit, dead, stretched and still, and as she went up to have a closer look at it she saw that it had its leg caught and broken in a trap.

'Poor thing!' she said, and bent down to see if she could release it, though it was too late to save it. She heard a steady scrunching of feet and, thinking it was Dan or Catherine come to find her, stood up to shout to them about the rabbit. But then the scruncher started to whistle; a jaunty grown-up whistle, and it was so long now since Tessa had seen another soul that she followed her first instinct, which was to duck out of sight behind a holly bush. She peered through the branches, curious and alarmed.

The whistling scruncher, then, was a young man of about twenty. She recognised him as a carpenter from the village. Dick, was it? Francis? Curiously, she had forgotten his name, though she could remember that he had made carts for her father, and that he was the best dancer in the street. He made chairs, too, she thought, and sold them to people in Sheffield, sometimes. Surely she would remember his name.

He was carrying a net over his shoulder. When he came to the trapped rabbit he laid the net down on the snow beside him and drew out a knife from the sheath in his belt. He knelt down to the trap and then suddenly stopped whistling. Tessa peeped round and

jerked her head back quickly. He was examining her
footprints in the snow. He straightened up and
followed the prints to the holly bush. Tessa could feel
his eyes probing the thickness of it. He spied her at
last and lunged round the side to grab her, quick as a
fox; but she was quicker. Like a frightened rabbit
herself she darted out of his reach and scuttled to the
shelter of another bush.

'Don't touch me!' she begged.

He stared at her, saw how she quivered, and how
wide with fear her eyes were. He dropped his hands to

his sides and squatted down again on his haunches as though to show her that he meant her no harm.

'What's tha name, child?'

'Tessa Tebbutt. And I know thee. Dick Mossop, as made our carts.'

'Tess Tebbutt? Is that right?' He looked in disbelief at her matted hair, her dress torn and undarned, the unwashed sheepskin round her back and on her feet; her face thin and pale and streaked with dirt. 'I wouldn't have known thee, Tess. But then I thought tha'd gone months since. Died. I thought all the Tebbutt children had died.'

'I'm with Catherine and Dan in the shepherd's barn.'

Dick whistled sharply, narrowing his eyes as though he still couldn't tell whether he really saw Tessa Tebbutt or not.

'In the top field barn, tha says? And wi'out tha mother and father?'

'My granma was ill. They couldn't come with us. I haven't seen my mother since ... before the snow. I haven't seen my father since ... since....' Tears blurted into her eyes as she sought in her confusion to remember how long ago it was that she last saw him. 'Since the day the wind blew.'

Dick whistled again. 'And art tha not afeard, up there?'

Tessa shook her head. She hadn't been afraid since the night Dan had heard Ghost, the mouse; not in the barn. She had been afraid by the river, when Mistress Hoggs had turned on them, and she had been afraid just now, when Dick had come. But the barn was home. 'Not afeard. But cold, at times. And hungry.'

'Aye. We're all hungry in the village, too,' Dick told her. 'I can't go into Sheffield to sell my chairs. No money, any of us. Nowhere to buy food, and the crops are running out. That's why I'm trapping rabbits, look.'

He went back to the rabbit and eased it out of its trap, while she watched him. 'But here. Take it,' and he thrust it towards her. 'Cook and eat it.'

She shrank away in horror. 'Nay, 'tis only just

dead. And besides …' she remembered. 'I mustn't touch it after thee.'

His first instinct was to fling the gift rabbit on to the ground. He turned to her, angry enough to shake her. Like Maggie Hoggs he resented the fact that the Tebbutt children had escaped into the hills. Why them, when his own little sister was sick with the fever at home? And yet he knew that if he could have spared his sister in just this way he would have done. And indeed, he told himself, why should the Tebbutt children suffer too, just because so many other children were sick and dying? So he turned his anger away from Tessa and on to the rabbit.

'Watch me,' he told her.

He slit its fur and peeled it away over the tucked legs, and slid the small shiny body out of it. He tossed the fur aside, like a rag. He looked up at Tessa who was absorbed. She sensed his anger, but didn't understand it; yet she was fascinated by his task.

'Well. And could tha do that, dost think?' He was gentle, now.

She nodded, scared. 'I think so.'

'Good.' He stood up and put the skinned rabbit in his net. 'That's how to get a rabbit ready for cooking. Tha's to get the middle of it out next, and I dare say tha could manage that an' all. Could tha?'

'Yes,' she whispered.

'Then I'll show thee where there's another rabbit trapped. Don't fret. I've not touched it, and I don't intend to.'

He strode off further up the hill, with Tessa running to keep up with him. When they came to the second trap he jerked his head towards it.

'If tha can hack that rabbit out, 'tis thine. And watch tha fingers, now. Then take it back to tha barn and skin it just as I've shown thee, and gut it, and tha'll get a fine broth from it. Does tha hear me?'

He knelt down a bit away from the trap and watched her while she worked the rabbit free. Her hands were shaking, both in fear of him and of touching the dead rabbit, but she daren't refuse. Besides, she could almost smell rabbit broth on the frosty air! He told her how to set the trap again.

'Well, now,' said Dick, gentle again, and thinking how like his little sister she was. 'This trap is for thee, and any rabbit tha finds in it is thine, from now on. I'll not touch it.'

'Thanks, Dick Mossop.' The rabbit hung from her grasp. She wanted to run away now. But – 'Dick,' she asked. 'Has tha seen my mother and father? Are they well?'

He was looking at his feet, and not at her. 'That I cannot tell thee. 'Tis the truth. Nobody leaves their houses now. I see no one. It seems that every house has someone sick in it. Nobody visits, for fear of taking and catching. I don't know, and that's the truth.'

She moved away from him, sick to the heart.

'But Tess, I've not heard anything bad about them. When there's real bad news, tha knows, usually the word gets round somehow.'

His words were as clumsy as wild pigs, he thought.

'But give me a message for them, and I'll take it to their cottage. I'll write it on a slate by their door, so they'll be sure to find it.'

'Oh, yes!' She searched her mind for something to tell them that they would want to know. There was so much. And so little.

'Well? What message shall I tell them?'

'Tell them ... tell them ... that Dan hurt his knee, but that 'tis better now.'

Dick smiled. 'I'll tell them that. And shall I tell them I gave thee a rabbit to cook?'

'Yes, please. And tell them we have sheepskins to keep us warm.'

'And if they leave a message out for thee, Tess, I'll bring it up.'

'I shall come here tomorrow, then, to see thee.'

'Do that.'

And off she ran with the rabbit light now in her hand, and her thoughts happy with the news she had for Catherine.

Dick watched her go, and then went back down to the village, wondering how he was going to tell his mother that he had only one rabbit for them instead of two.

But it was a house of sickness that he went home to, and though Tessa came back to that spot in the woods for many days to come, she never saw the young carpenter Dick Mossop again.

9. The End of the Dancing

Catherine and Dan had long since returned to the barn to put dry clothes on. Catherine wanted to get the fire burning and the pot boiling before the day's brightness turned to damp. It was Dan's turn to see to it. He crouched over it, warming his hands and his face by the flame, listening to the close crackle of the kindling twigs and the distant harsh clatter of crows in flight to the dark woods. His thoughts were miles away.

Tessa could see the glow of the fire as she came back across the moor to their field, and as she climbed the mound she could see Dan, his black figure bending to scoop up twigs and sticks and heap them into the heart of the flames to make their redness burst. The snow on the earth round him was almost blue, except for the touch of yellow from the firelight, and the sky was rushing into blackness. The barn glowed, warm and welcome, with the small light inside the door.

'Oh, who will light my fire,
Oh, who will sweep my floor,
Oh, who will wear the pretty cloak
That hangs behind the door....'

she sang softly, remembering the ballad that their
mother used to sing. Dan broke away from his reverie
at the sound of the familiar song and the echoes it
brought to him of home.

'Where's tha been, Tess, all this time? And what's
tha got?'

'Shush! 'Tis a surprise. Build us a good fire. We'll
eat well tonight.'

Tessa went into the barn and laid the rabbit on the
table-stone. Catherine had been sorting out vegetables for a broth.

'Wherever did tha find that?' she marvelled. She
turned the rabbit over gently, not afraid of the dead
thing as Tessa had been.

Tessa jigged about with excitement as she told her
sister about Dick Mossop, and the message he was to
take from them to their farm, and his promise that
they could have any rabbits they found in the far trap.
And Catherine remembered how she'd danced with
Dick Mossop only last Michaelmas, and how
everyone had clapped, not just because he was such a
fine dancer, either. She remembered the grey frock
that her mother had made her for that day, and the
violet ribbons that her father had brought her for her
hair, and, though she didn't tell Tessa and Dan, she

remembered that Dick Mossop had told her that the colour of the ribbons had matched her eyes.

'Did he ask about me?'

'Not in particular. Why should he, anyway?' Tessa was keen to get started on the rabbit.

'Here,' she handed Catherine the best knife. 'Nick the fur for me, just below the leg.'

'And then what?'

'Then I'll skin it and gut it for the pot, but I daren't make the first cut.'

'Skin it and gut it! Tha don't know how!'

'I know how!' Tessa was indignant. 'Dick Mossop showed me how, so there.'

'Well. So. I know how an' all. I'll do it.'

Catherine lifted the knife and was about to slide it into the creature's side, but her hand stayed still.

'I dare do it,' offered Dan, who had come in to see what all the fun was about.

'Nay. Leave off. I'll do it.' But still Catherine's hand dropped away from the rabbit.

It was Tessa who saw her misery. She took the knife from her limp hand and laid it on the table-stone, then she put her arm round her sister and drew her down on to the thinking-log.

'Cathy. Please don't fret. 'Tis only an old rabbit.'

'I know that.'

'And tha's been so brave, and kept us going all these weeks and months. Must tha cry over an old rabbit that's going in the stewpot?'

Catherine shook her head. Her face was streaked

where she'd wiped her tears away with her grimy sleeve. Dick Mossop would never have recognised her now, if he thought of her at all.

''Tis not that, Tess. Not the rabbit.'

'What, then?'

''Tis the thought of Mother, and our house, and working with her in our kitchen to get the food ready, like we used to do. I want to go home.'

But she cheered up later when Tessa had skinned the rabbit and made it ready for the pot, and she felt better still when she could smell it cooking in the pot of vegetables.

They stood round the fire to eat it, nursing the hot bowls of broth in their hands. The dark sky was spiked with stars. They could hear beasts howling miles away on the hills, in other valleys, but they weren't afraid of them. They could face anything now, Catherine thought, when the warmth of the meal crept through her body and filled her with well-being. Things would be all right. They would bide their time, and all would be well for them.

But they were tiny black figures on the huge whitened earth. The small fire soon burnt itself out. The meal was soon eaten. Then the noises of the night started up again to alarm them. Then, indeed, the little barn seemed a small place to shelter in.

Sometimes, when the door was fastened up against the night, there was singing and dancing in the barn. It was always Tessa who started it, sometimes to send

Dan off to sleep, but at times just because she couldn't help it; she never seemed to be low-spirited for long. Her best song was about the spiders that dropped down from the rafters and loped across to lurk in the straw.

'They wait there till we're asleep, then come out to tickle us,' she said.

> 'When Dan lies asleeping
> Asleeping in the night,
> Up comes the spider,
> Up he jumps in fright.
> "A ghost!" he cries.
> "A leggy ghost,
> With hairy fingers waving . . ."'

She would drape a sack over her head, and crawl along towards Dan, with long straws sticking down from her hands. Dan found a stick to beat against the side of the table-stone, and Catherine tied knives into the straining bag, and shook them to jangle like bells, and then Tessa would dance closer and closer to the candle-flame so that her shadow grew long and black on the walls and ceiling of the barn.

Their dancing was so loud one night that the beating on the door seemed at first to be part of it.

'Hush,' said Dan suddenly. 'Listen.'

They all stopped.

Rap. Rap. Rap. Knuckles on wood. The children froze into silence.

Again: Rap. Rap. Rap.

' 'Tis the messenger!' Dan shouted, and ran to pull back the door.

A man was standing there, half-leaning against the door, and as it opened he slumped down in the doorway. He rolled a little way to the side and settled down on to the snow, as if to sleep.

' 'Tis Clem!' said Dan.

Catherine slammed the door shut again and stood with her back to it. Dan and Tessa were slow to grasp what had happened. They tried to pull her away so that they could open up the door again.

'Catherine. Bring him in. 'Tis Clem.'

'I daren't,' she said.

'But Cathy!' Dan tried to heave her away. 'He's my friend.'

'Tha saw his face,' said Catherine. 'He's sick.'

'Then tha *must* let him in,' pleaded Tessa.

'Doesn't tha understand!' Catherine refused to be pulled away.

' 'Tis thee as doesn't understand!' said Dan. 'He's Clem. He lives here. He's sick, Catherine. Let him in.'

'Think!' said Catherine. 'Think! If he is sick, then he may have the plague.'

Tessa understood at last. 'But we can't just leave him there, Cathy.'

'What else can we do?' The question was hopeless. 'What would Mother do?'

'Tha knows very well what Mother would do,' said Dan indignantly. 'She'd bring him in and give him a good supper, an' look after him till he was better, even if she didn't know him.'

Catherine sighed. If only it was as simple as that. 'Well. Is the broth still warm?'

Tessa could have hugged her sister. 'It soon can be. The fire won't be out yet; I can bring up the heat again. Shall I do it now?'

Catherine nodded and stood back to let her pull the door open. 'Keep away from Clem, though,' she whispered. She held on to Dan's hand firmly.

Clem was standing up now. In the sharp light of the moon they could see how bright his eyes were, and how his face was blistered with sweat. He didn't even seem to notice Tessa as she moved in front of him to the fire to rekindle its flame under the cooking-pot.

Dan would have run to him all right. 'Clem,' he said. The man looked at him but didn't seem to know him.

'I came back here to be alone,' he said. 'I don't know what to do with myself.' He staggered down on to his knees, too weak to stay standing.

Catherine had seen sick sheep do this. It was all she could do to stop herself from running forward to catch him. She knew that was what her mother would have done. She'd have kept him warm, and fed him, of course she would, but she would also have kept him away from the children. Would she really have sent them away from home and made them face out a winter in a cold barn if she'd known that something like this would happen? She must do what her mother would do, then.

She pulled Dan back into the barn with her. 'He'll be all right, Dan,' she said firmly. 'Stay here now.' She brought out her own rug from the straw and laid it over Clem.

'The broth is ready,' called Tessa.

'Bring it in the small bowl,' said Catherine. 'Put it down by him.'

Tessa brought the steaming bowl over carefully. 'Here, Clem,' she said, putting the bowl near his face where he could smell the thick soup. ' 'Tis hot, mind, and good for thee.'

To Catherine's relief Clem managed to raise himself up so that he was leaning on one elbow. He pulled himself against the side of the barn, where he could sit comfortably, and sipped greedily at the broth.

' 'Tis good,' he said thickly. 'Bless thee for this.'

'Come in, now,' said Catherine to Tessa. 'We must talk. Leave him to finish that.'

They went back into the barn and closed the door behind them. Catherine was almost too wrapped up in worry to speak. If only there was something to tell her what she must do now. Without realising it she had sat herself down on the thinking-log and had picked up the slate, and was drawing letters on it absently. Dan and Tessa sat down with her and watched her quietly. Their father would be like this, lost in thought, before he spoke to his family of his problems. They must wait, then.

'I want to help Clem,' she said at last. 'And yet I want to do what Mother wanted, and save us all. Save thee.'

They said nothing; Dan because he didn't understand, and Tessa because the problem was too big.

'If we bring Clem in here, and he does have the plague, then we may catch it, too. We may die of it.'

'We needn't touch him, though,' said Tessa. 'He could lie over there, away from us.'

'But we'd be breathing the air he breathes,' insisted Catherine. She shuddered, remembering what Maggie Hoggs had said to them. 'I don't know what spreads this plague from one person to another, but I do know that when he sneezes he puts it into the air. We mustn't ever go that close to him. I won't let thee.'

'So what do we do? We can't leave him out there. I think we should risk it, and make him better.' Tessa jumped up. 'Come on, Cath. Let's do that.'

'I know what we can do,' said Dan, but Catherine ignored him. She ran to the door before Tessa could reach it.

'Clem,' she called. 'Can tha hear me?'

'Aye,' he said, and his voice sounded much stronger now.

'Has tha been down to the village?'

'I have. I went down there to see our Moll.'

'Did tha see anyone – did tha see the people at Tebbutt's farm?'

Clem coughed. The three children were kneeling down behind the door, straining to catch his voice. 'I saw no one. Doors and shutters closed. No one on the streets. No one in the fields. No voices – nobody, nothing. I thought I were sleeping. I've never come on owt like that before. I went on down to our Moll's house, and tha knows what Moll's like – she's one for singing, she is.'

Catherine nodded. Molly Carter, Clem's sister, was their mother's friend, a big, rosy woman with a loud voice; a bit noisy at times, her mother used to say; the sort of person you couldn't be doing with first thing in the morning.

'Well, there wasn't a sound coming from her house when I got there. And those children of hers, like a herd of fresh goats, shouting and banging and climbing up me as if I was a tree in a field – not a sign of them. I went in, thinking to find a feast ready, because there's always food at Moll's house. Table were set, mind, and I sat meself down to tuck in, thinking they were gone to market or some such. Why – milk was blue in cup. Bread were stale as stones. And then I heard our Moll, upstairs, crying.'

He started coughing and sneezing again. Tessa fetched the candle over from the table-stone, so its light would give them some comfort.

'What happened, Clem?' prompted Catherine.

'Our Moll was alone in the house, and she was alone because those three children of hers were all dead, and her husband was out digging the ground for a place to put them in. I went to comfort her, and she screamed at me to get away from her, and save myself at least. It was too late for her, she said. She locked herself into her room and I knew she was right. I gave her my

99

blessing and grabbed my bits and pieces from the table and ran for my life out of the village. I never want to go back down there again. And then, yesterday it may have been, I started with this fever. Maybe I can shake it off, I thought, if I get to shelter in the barn. But how was I to know there'd be three children here?'

His words sank away from them. The children sat for a long time in their crouched positions by the door. What Clem had told them, then, was the thing that their mother had dreaded above everything else, and that she'd done so much to avoid. He had brought the plague from their village to the barn.

10. Another Mouth to Feed

All the time Clem was talking, Dan was trying to get Catherine's attention. He took the slate from her and began to draw, as she had done, and when he had finished he handed it to her, almost too excited to speak.

'See, Cath! I know what we can do!'

She looked at his drawing of the barn, not understanding.

'See!' Impatiently he drew in some figures. Three stick figures in the barn. One stick animal. Two stick birds. And round the back of the barn, where he had sketched in the pen, a stick man, lying down. 'There!'

'Dan!' She thrust the slate to Tessa. The sheep-pen of course was ideal. Part of it they had already covered with logs and sacking to keep the wood for the fire dry. They would bring the wood into the barn, and Cloudy and the hens.

'We'll make a stable of the barn, and never mind the smell!' said Catherine. 'And we can light a small fire in the pen, where there's no cover, to keep him warm

and to keep the animals away. And he can have my
sack.'

They ran about their task, carrying in huge arm-
loads of wood which they piled up by the thinking-
log. Then they led in Cloudy, who immediately began
to eat the straw in the barn. The hens clucked busily
after her, pecking up the grains that were lying round
the corn bins, then fluttered up on to the straw-pile
and found themselves hollows. Catherine did what

she could to clean out the pen while Dan and Tessa brought out straw for Clem to lie on, and another sack. While they were doing this Clem sat huddled up against the barn wall with Catherine's blanket round him, and when it was all prepared he half-walked, half-crawled round the back and into the pen. He snuggled himself thankfully into the straw, and drew the second rug round himself.

Tessa filled his bowl again from another bowl, and put it just within his reach. There could be no water for him; the trickle-stream was still frozen. Tomorrow they would follow it down to where it was wider and maybe thawed.

Catherine hovered anxiously just outside the pen. 'I'm right sorry, Clem. It looks as if we've pinched tha shelter.'

He didn't answer.

'We've done the best we can for thee.'

Clem coughed into the straw; it seemed to wrack his body. He drew the rugs back round himself, and lay back again. 'Tis good. I thank thee for this.' And then he seemed to sleep.

Dan had the idea of dragging the remains of the fire round to the mouth of the pen. It would bring a little warmth, though it would hardly last the night out. They were careful to place it where the smoke wouldn't annoy Clem and where sparks wouldn't land on straw. They'd learnt to take this sort of care during the last few weeks. They could see now by the glow from the fire that Clem wasn't asleep but lay watching them, too weary to move or speak. And they were weary themselves; they hadn't worked as hard or as fast as this since they first moved up to the barn.

Satisfied, then, that they had done as much as they could for Clem that night, they gave him their good-night blessings and left him to try to sleep.

'I pray that it restores him,' said Tessa. 'Let's go to sleep ourselves now, before Cloudy eats up all our beds of straw!'

It was good to wake up the next morning and hear the hens fussing about in the straw by their heads. Cloudy lowed across to the children as though welcoming their morning chatter. Poor Dan had the job of cleaning out the space where she had spent the night and laying a sprinkling of fresh straw down for her while Tessa led her out to milk her, not that she gave much that was worth having just now. They had decided that what she did yield would be given to Clem, if he could manage it. Catherine ran round to peep in at him. He was awake, and lying in much the same position as he'd been in when they'd left him the night before. He told her that he was much rested.

He managed to push out his bowl, and Catherine drew it towards her with a stick, and ladled snow in it to clean it out. She built another fire away from the pen to boil the gruel, and she poured some of Cloudy's sweet warm milk into that, and pushed it back towards Clem. Clem managed to swallow a little of it. Then she burnt the stick.

Day by day Clem seemed to grow a little stronger, though from time to time his fever came back and left him pale and exhausted. He talked to them when he was well, and he referred again and again to the day he had last seen his sister down in their village.

'I shouldn't have left her,' he said bitterly. 'What if she's alone now, and in need of nursing?'

'Well, tha couldn't have nursed her, anyway,' Tessa reminded him from her perch on the sitting-stone. 'Tha can't even stand upright, let alone do any nursing.'

'When I'm better,' he said, 'I'll go back down and see her.'

That thought would comfort him a little, and he'd doze away for a time. And then, when the sunlight fell across his face, he would stir from his sleep, remembering a task that was to be done. 'Has the year turned yet?' he would ask. They felt it had. The days were longer, it seemed, and the sun was not so pale. But surely if the spring had come then all the snows on the moors would be gone; the trickle-stream wouldn't be frozen first thing.

On days like this Clem would come staggering out to the mouth of his pen, shielding his eyes against the day's brightness.

'I must get up to my sheep. What have they done for their winter feeding? They'll be lambing soon, and then what?'

Tessa, alarmed, would shout for Catherine to come, and Clem would flop to his knees in a faint, and it would be all he could do to drag himself back to his bed again.

'And stay there, an' all!' Tessa would say to him in her mother's voice. 'We'll have none of this capering!'

In her heart Tessa worried about Clem. He seemed to make progress; he ate a little each day, but he was listless and weak still.

'Dost think Clem's better yet?' she asked Catherine one morning. They were lying wrapped in their blankets, and could tell by the way their breath hung in the air that it was far too cold yet to get up.

'I can't tell. Maybe he'll know when he's better, and just go.'

'Ah. I don't want him to go,' said Dan.

'He changes so quickly,' said Tessa. 'Sometimes he's in such a fury with himself that I think the pen will fall apart with his twisting. And then sometimes he lies so quiet and still that I can't tell whether he's awake or asleep or . . .'

'He isn't strong enough to feed himself,' said Catherine quickly. 'He needs someone to lift the bowl to his lips for him.'

'But most of all he's lonely. Sometimes I feel I would just like to sit by him, and talk, and hold his hand.'

'What for?' asked Dan.

'For comfort,' Tessa said. 'But I daren't.'

'Comfort!' said Catherine. 'That's the one thing we can't give him.'

Dan was the first up next morning. He came back into the barn soon after daylight and knelt by the two girls, flicking water in their faces from the little bowl he was holding.

'Goblin!' shrieked Catherine. 'Little toad! Stop it!'

'But see what it is.' He held out the bowl to her.

'I see what it is, all right. 'Tis water, fool, and cold water at that. It bites as though it has teeth in it, 'tis that cold.'

'I got it from the trickle-stream.'

'Tha never did. 'Tis frozen solid,' said Tessa.

''Tis thawed, Tess! Look – the ice has all gone!'

Dan ran back to the door and pulled it open. Sunlight like gold blazed through, so they could see dust motes dancing in it; they could hear from behind the barn the rapid splash of water from the trickle-stream, and that was a sound that they'd long forgotten about.

'We must take Clem some fresh water,' said Catherine.

'I took him some already. He said 'twas better than ale, and sweeter.'

Tessa led Cloudy out and tethered her to her tree. The two hens, long ago nicknamed Dame Cluck and Mistress Feathers, squawked after her.

'We'll expect good milk from thee now,' she said. 'And an egg or two from tha friends.'

Later that morning the two girls decided to go up to the trap. Maybe the sunshine had brought the beasts out from their winter holes, and there'd be a rabbit caught there for them.

There was not. 'No matter,' said Catherine. 'There's still some salt-beef left.' And they both laughed, because they'd grown to hate the stuff. They wandered further down into the woods, not noticing till they came out again into a clearing that the sky was clouding over and that the sunlight had gone.

'It may rain before we get back,' Catherine said. 'And I thought spring was come.'

'It has!' said Tessa. 'Look under the trees.'

Thrusting up through the thickness of grass and roots they found snowdrops, lovely. They made the girls feel as though winter was lifting itself off the earth.

'Let's take some back,' Tessa said. 'And thread them in the straw to make the barn look nice.'

'We will look well in our lovely house!' laughed Catherine. 'Flowers in it, and a cow!'

'No doubt the cow will eat the flowers, an' all, as a change from eating up our bed. Shall we go back now, Cath? The sun's gone.'

But Catherine wanted to go further on down into the woods; it was the first time they'd wandered far from the barn since the snow came. It was good to get away from it for a time, and from their worries about Clem. Strangely, she felt that things were getting better now; but maybe it was the glimpse of sunshine and the show of snowdrops that made her feel that way.

'Let's walk a bit further,' she said. 'Just to enjoy the

day. Dan will be all right.'

Dan was on the sitting-stone outside the barn, drawing on his slate. He was aware of sounds coming from the pen but ignored them at first, thinking that Clem was cleaning out his bed area to make himself more comfortable, as he sometimes did now. Then he heard Clem groan. He ran to the pen and peered in. Clem was lying in the straw, twisting and thrashing about in it in what seemed to be an agony. Again and again he raised his head up, only to let it drop back into the straw. Dan watched him in horror. He had never seen Clem in this state before.

'Clem! Are tha badly? What can I fetch thee?'

But Clem didn't answer him; for that matter, didn't even seem to hear him. Dan dropped the slate which he'd been clutching still and ran like a hare across the field, over the wall, and across the moor to the woods.

'Cathy! Tessa!' he shouted, sending the crows up in alarm from their branches. He saw no sign of the two girls. He ran as far as the trap, but they'd long since gone from there. Just as wildly he ran back to the pen, and edged himself as close as he dared to the fevered Clem.

'Shall I fetch thee water?' he whispered.

Clem gasped something that could have been yes, and half-opened his eyes. Dan picked up the bowl and ran to the trickle-stream, hastily scooped up water, and ran back to the pen.

'Here, Clem.'

He stood watching the shepherd doubtfully. The man's skin gleamed with sweat. Dan edged the bowl to him but Clem didn't even see it.

'I don't want thee to be ill, Clem. Please don't. Please don't do that.'

It seemed to Dan the longest moment of his life, till he decided what he must do. He crept into the pen and sat down in the straw beside Clem. Then he took the bowl up, raised Clem's head into his lap, and moistened his dry lips with water.

Tessa and Catherine had come down to the edge of the wood. From here they could see the river, brown and swollen with thaw. They could hear the rush of it as it swept across the stepping-stones.

Catherine grasped Tessa's arm. 'I can see smoke, look. Lot's of it.' They craned forward, trying to see beyond Hoggs' farm and the trees beyond that to the chimneys of the lower village – the smoke seemed to gust, much greater in volume than chimney smoke, yet it was impossible to tell where it was coming from. And from far away, it seemed, came the high babble of voices.

'What's happening?' asked Tessa. 'Shall we go on down, just to the river, to see what it is?'

'I don't know. I don't think we would see more than we can see from up here.'

'But please!' Tessa started to run down ahead of her. 'Before it rains!' The sky was growing heavier now, and there was that still kind of echo in the air that comes just before heavy rain. And just as they came to the edge of the river the first bloated drops began to to fall.

Clem was calmer now, and seemed to be drifting off into a sleep. Dan settled him down into the straw and crawled out of the pen to fill up his bowl with fresh water. The rain soaked him before he reached the trickle-stream.

'I needn't have brought it this far,' he told himself. 'Next time I'll just shove it outside the pen, and the rain will fill it up.'

By the time he reached the pen again his shirt was drenched. Clem was awake, staring at him with unseeing eyes.

'I'm as wet as a fish, Clem,' said Dan. 'But tha's hotter than fire, poor Clem.'

He stripped off his wet shirt and rolled it up, and then used it to wipe the sweat away from Clem's forehead and neck. He could see how comforting the cool cloth was to the man.

Clem drifted back into sleep, for just a few minutes, and when he woke up again his eyes were clear. He looked up at the boy for a long time, taking him in, taking in where he was, and what he was doing there with him.

'God bless thee for this,' he whispered.

'Are tha better?'

Clem closed his eyes as if to sleep again. 'Much

better. But I must ask thee to go, Dan. Now. And never, never, come in here to me again.'

Dan stared at him. The chill in Clem's voice made the hairs on the back of his neck creep. Why wouldn't Clem look at him again? He shivered violently; cold, and fright, and a sudden release of tension after nursing Clem through his fever taking a hold of him together. He crawled out to the mouth of the pen, and, without even a backward glance at Clem, flung himself out into the lashes of rain and dashed round to the front of the barn. He was shaking in convulsions, colder than he'd ever been before. His old shirt was hanging over the beam at the back of the barn. He rubbed himself down with it, put it on, damp as it was, and crawled like a sick cat into his sack in the straw. He buried himself down inside it for warmth, stuck his thumb in his mouth, and at last fell asleep.

11. Candle-light Vigil

The bonfire in the village was burning down, spluttering to nothing under the deluge. The chairs and beds that had been heaped up on to it caved in towards each other, black skeletons with thrusting arms, and sagged into the low heart of the flames. Black ashes mounted the air and plunged down again with the rain. Smoke billowed dismally. Yet still the villagers hung round the fire, reluctant to leave it till they'd seen their own furniture burnt down, reluctant to leave the gossip of friends that they'd missed for months. Yet at last they did leave, defeated by the downpour, and sought shelter in each others' houses.

Tessa and Catherine saw nothing of this, though they too were defeated by the rain and scurried back up the long slope into the woods. They stayed there, sheltering as best as they could, and gradually moved higher up the woods, dodging from tree to tree like squirrels. Rain thundered down from the branches into their hair and down their necks. They slithered on the wet

grasses as they ran. At the moor edge they waited.

'Let's run for the barn,' said Catherine.

'Yes,' agreed Tessa. 'Let's make a dash for it. We can't stay here, anyway. We'll drown.'

When at last they reached the barn they saw that Dan was asleep in the straw. They crept round, not wanting to disturb him, flinging off their wet clothes and putting on the dry things that were hanging on the low beam.

'No rabbit broth to eat today,' whispered Tessa.

'The fire wouldn't have lit, anyway. Never mind – here's a fine piece of salt-beef for thee, instead.'

'I'd rather eat a dog than salt-beef!'

'Aye. So would I. How about an apple, then?'

The bin of apples was nearly empty, and the fruit in it was shrivelled and dusty. They sat on the thinking-log to munch them and to chew at the tedious salt-beef. The candle-flame guttered low as a draught blew in from somewhere.

'There's a wind getting up,' said Catherine. 'The barn will creak like an old boat tonight.'

She lit a fresh candle. 'Only a couple left now,' she said. 'We must make more from the old stubs.'

'Tomorrow,' said Tessa.

'Aye. Tomorrow.'

The wind got up during the night. They listened to its moaning, and snuggled up together for comfort. Dan slept fitfully, and didn't even know that the girls had returned. In their haste to get back in from the rain the girls had forgotten to bring in Cloudy and the two hens, and at first light the cow broke away from her tethering and started off across the field. She struggled up the mound and padded across the moorland. The hens bowed their heads against the wind and scuttled after her. In delicate slow file they moved into the woods, down and down the steep path, across the bottom clearing and over to the stepping-stones. Back to the ample feeding of their own fields.

Catherine was first up. She found some of yesterday's gruel in the pot and decided to carry the whole thing out to pour into Clem's bowl, and then to try to get a small fire going to make some more. The rain had stopped, but the wind was so strong that it nearly drove her back into the barn again when she opened the door.

' 'Tis like pushing against a wild pony,' she gasped.

'Leave it.' Tessa, drowsy still in her sack, was in no mind to get up yet.

'I must see to Clem. And we need milk soon, for our own gruel. Get up, Tess, and wake Dan, too. We need more wood fetching soon, if this wind lets us get out.' She pushed herself out and let the door swing back behind her.

Grumbling, Tessa felt her way out on to the cold floor. She leaned over to shake Dan, but he huddled inside his sack.

'Go away.'

'No. If I've got to get up, then so have thee. There's things to do today. And we must eat soon.'

'I don't want to eat. I'm not hungry.'

'I've heard that before, Dan Tebbutt. As soon as food's cooked, tha'll come begging, I know thee! Come on, snail.' She shook him again. 'Why, tha's as hot as fire, Dan.'

'Leave me, Tessa. My head hurts.'

116

His eyes were bright. Tessa put the cover blanket back round him, and went out quietly to do her work. Dan sneezed into the straw and, shivering, drew himself down into the warmth of the bed.

Tessa battled round the barn against the wind in her search for Cloudy. 'Cloudy!' she called. 'Where's tha gone, tha daft cow?' Cloudy had never wandered from the barn before, and Tessa felt guilty for not bringing her in the night before when the rains came. It was Cloudy who brought them the smells and the comfort of home every day. She felt now as if she'd lost a good friend. ''Tis only an old cow,' she told herself, and 'Cloudy! Cloudy! Please come back!' she called. At last, and with a sure dread in her heart that Cloudy had gone for good, she made her way back to the barn.

Catherine was back already, crouched over on the thinking-log with her head in her hands. She looked up when Tessa came in, and each knew by the other's face that something dreadful had happened.

'Cloudy's gone,' said Tessa simply.

'Aye. And so has Clem.'

Tears sprang into Tessa's eyes. 'Clem?' She crossed herself quickly, out of respect for him. 'Poor Clem.'

'Nay, I don't mean that; leastways I hope 'tis not that. He's left us, Tess.'

'*Left* us! But how? He can hardly walk.'

'Then he's crawled away in the night.'

'Why would he want to do that?'

'Tessa, stop asking me. I don't know! He's gone, that's all I know.' In her heart she thought about sick animals crawling away to die; under bushes and by the side of hedges.

'Maybe he's gone down to the village again to be with his sister.'

'Aye. Maybe so. But look at this. This is what worries me more.'

She held up a crumpled white garment. 'Dan's shirt, look. I found it in the place where Clem was lying.'

Tessa's heart beat like a bird in her throat. 'He told me he felt sick this morning,' she whispered. 'And he's hot.'

Dan was awake, listening to them. 'And my head hurts, Tess,' he reminded her.

'But 'tis the first time any of us has been ill,' Tessa said brightly. 'And surely spring is on its way. We can fight silly things like headaches, can't we, Dan?'

'It hurts a lot.'

'I know,' she said. 'Ssh. I know.'

'Don't tha know how serious this is?' snapped Catherine. 'How did tha shirt get there?'

Dan puckered his face. He wanted to be left alone. 'Clem was in a fever. I left it for him to cool his face and hands with.'

'Tha threw it in to him, didn't tha?' Catherine nodded to Dan as though urging him to agree with her.

He tried to remember the scene in the pen. He could picture Clem's eyes, bright as water. He could see his tongue, darting like a lizard to lick his dry lips. 'He was in a fever,' he repeated. 'I held his head up so he could drink, and then I wiped his face with my wet shirt.'

Catherine let the shirt drop down into the dust. 'Don't tha know what tha've done! After everything we said to thee? Why did tha do it?'

Her anger and fear frightened Dan. 'I wanted to comfort him,' he said in a small, scared voice.

At least Tessa understood him. She hugged him to her, though her throat was tight with tears. 'Good boy. We'll soon have thee well again. Tha's braver than us, tha knows. We'll get thee well.'

Dan allowed himself to be hugged. He could remember his mother doing this. He would like to be back home now with his mother and father. The barn was draughty. The creaking in the rafters annoyed him. The wind howled like a ghost outside, and the chill sound of it made a pain come up behind his eyes. His throat felt raw and swollen.

'Can we go home?' he asked.

'We will. Right soon. Get well first, Dan. Try to sleep now. There, try to sleep.'

Tessa's soothing voice brought Catherine back from the pit of fear her thoughts had plunged her into. Dan would need feeding and nursing to bring him through this. She sorted through the bins – a few vegetables left, a handful of grains of corn, an elbow of salt-beef. Was that all? Never mind, she could make a good broth with it now, and perhaps soon there would be a rabbit in the trap for them. They'd manage. Things would get better. They couldn't come as far as this and give up at the first sign of illness, could they? What would her mother say!

She put the bits of food into a pot and took a taper from the candle. 'More candles to make,' she reminded herself as she hurried out. She kept the taper inside the pot against the wind and hurried round to the pen. There was no need to be careful now. She lit a fire in the pen where it was sheltered from the wind, and brought water from the trickle-stream. Soon the broth was bubbling and her hands and face at least were warm as she crouched over the flames. Round the side of the barn the tall trees crashed their great heads together. Grey clouds ballooned across the sky. The gorse flattened itself in the wind's rush. Catherine felt her mind turning and turning in the centre of the gale, listening to a sound that seemed to take her away to another time; that seemed to bring memories of calm and comfort down from the great slabs of rock that protected their barn, and the hill, and the valley below, and the blighted village; that always would protect them, ages from now.

'My brains must be freezing in my head!' she thought, 'to give me ideas like this! The future frightens me, right enough. I must think of now, and getting our Dan better, and keeping Tessa and me well, an' all. What's the future to do with me?'

And she hurried back into the barn with the pot

steaming and bubbling in her hands.

Dan wasn't interested in the broth. Tessa took some to try to coax him: 'A taste for me, and a taste for thee!' as their mother used to do, but he hardly sniffed at it when the bowl touched his lips. Catherine was sick with worry, and couldn't touch it. 'But we must eat, all of us,' she sighed. 'We need to keep strong now.'

'Tomorrow,' promised Tessa. Then she sang Dan some of her best songs, but there was no dancing that night.

Catherine, on the thinking-log, fought to keep away the black thoughts that clustered like moths in her mind. 'Be busy! Be busy!' she said to herself, and it was her mother's voice saying it. Don't have time to be sad. So she set to work scraping together the blobs of wax that had run from the candles into the hole in the table-stone. She grated up the stubs of candles and melted them in a bowl, with a piece of plaited sacking strands in that for a wick. The last of the old candles was burning away. She scooped it out and let it drop into the bowl too, though it stank and smarted her eyes. At last the new candle was lit. She was pleased with her work.

'The light hurts my eyes,' said Dan. 'Please move it, Cathy.'

So she placed the bowl on the ground, behind the table-stone, so only the yellow glow from the light could be seen. Huge shadows leapt like goblins across the ceiling as the draught from under the door made the flame flatten and twist. Dan hid his head in Tessa's side. She stroked his hair, and the low sound of her singing soon drifted him to sleep. Catherine stayed on the thinking-log, lost now for tasks, but afraid to go to sleep. How long would it be, she wondered, before the fever took over Dan's little body with its terrible strength? And then what? The sleep of peace that would take him away from them for ever?

And then what? Tessa, who wouldn't leave his side.

And then herself.

'Please God, no,' she murmured. 'People *do* get better. Let him get better.'

She made herself think of spring, and collecting primroses from the woods to bring into the barn. She thought of finding mushrooms in the dewy grass, and cooking them on their fire before the sun was fully risen. And she thought of nesting swallows busy in the rafters of their barn; making their home there.

But it was hard to think these thoughts with the wind shrieking like a mad thing outside and the black shadows thrown by the candle stretching and leaping like the fingers of the night on the walls of the barn, and Dan shivering in his straw.

Slowly, slowly, her eyes began to close.

'Cathy! The light's gone out!' It was Tessa's voice that woke her, and for a second she stared into the suffocating blackness, not breathing, and knew that the wind had stopped breathing too.

Then came a pounding on the shutters of the barn

123

that shocked her into full wakefulness.

'Will it be Clem?' Tessa whispered.

Catherine's head was clamouring with thoughts.

The pounding came again, fit to waken the dead. 'Children! Open up! Let me in! The plague is over!'

'Listen to him, Catherine!' Tessa was shaking her as if to shake her dreams away. ' 'Tis the messenger Mother promised us. The plague is over!'

But it was Dan who struggled out of his sack and ran to try to pull the shutters back. Catherine, not even fighting back her tears, ran to try to help him.

'The plague is over!' called the man again – and from somewhere long ago, Catherine knew his voice.

12. Coming Back

At last the shutters were pulled back. Sunlight streamed through. Outside stood their father, smiling in at them, and behind him they could see their mother, breathless after her long steep climb up the hill from the village.

'Come on, then,' their father said. 'The storm's over.'

Catherine, dazed, looked round at her brother and sister. They stood hand in hand, watching her silently, as if waiting for some signal from her.

'It's time to go back,' she said.

'What have you been doing in there?' Mum said. 'Good grief, kids, what are you wearing!'

'We were doing a play,' said Patsy, struggling out of the sacks and sheepskins. 'Catherine told us a story and we were acting it out. We put our wet things on the beam to dry.'

She brought their cagoules and jeans over to the other two. They were dry. In silence Catherine picked up the discarded sheepskins and laid them under the

straw, and laid the sacks in a pile at the side.

Dad pushed another sack through the shutters to her. 'I met the old fellow coming down the hill. He said thank you very much for these, and he had a good rest.'

'Fancy not letting him, in, though, when it's his barn,' Mum laughed.

'You told us not to let anyone in,' Patsy reminded her. 'Didn't she, Cathy?'

Andrew sneezed. 'Sounds as if you've caught cold, my lad,' said Mum. 'And I'm not surprised with that soaking you've had.'

'Your Gran's full of cold too,' Dad said. 'She's had

a job shaking it off. But she'll be all the better for seeing you three, so get a move on! Quick!'

Laughing, Patsy and Andrew pulled back the door and ran out into the sunshine. Catherine followed them to the doorway, and looked back. She could see a mound of fresh straw, stored for the winter. She could see a row of bins, empty, against the wall. She could see a log, and a large stone. She heard a scratching sound, and maybe, somewhere, it was a mouse scrabbling.

But then the old cruck barn was still and silent and empty. None of its shadows moved.

'Catherine Tebbutt ... bids thee ... farewell.'

She closed the door behind her, and raced like a mad thing over the field after the others.

'Wait for me!' she shouted. 'I'm coming home.'